THE DEVILS
STAIR CASE

A Pegasus Investigations Mystery

By Brian D. Eyre

Swinging Cats and Blinking Hats Press
Dallas, Texas

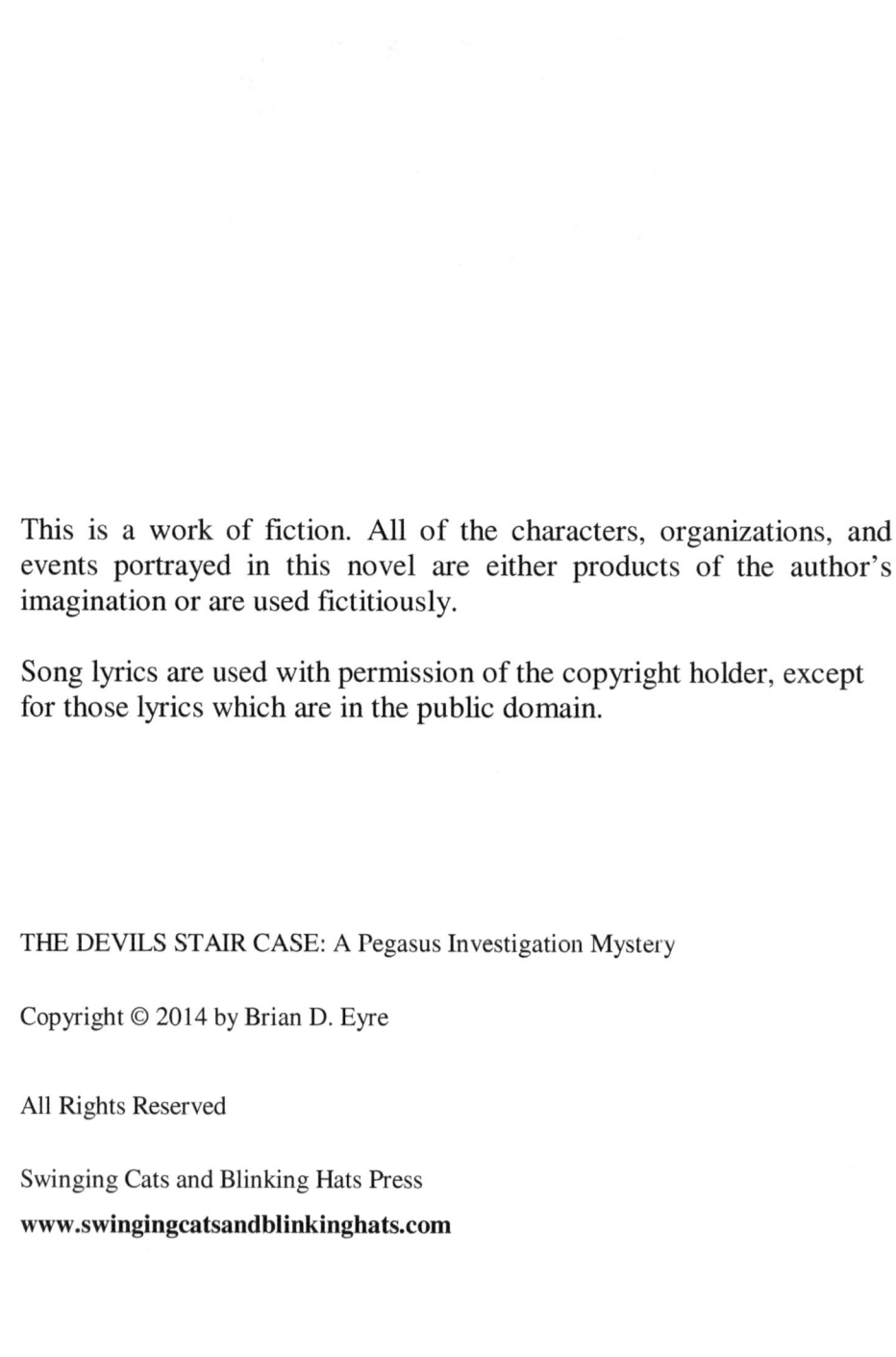

This is a work of fiction. All of the characters, organizations, and events portrayed in this novel are either products of the author's imagination or are used fictitiously.

Song lyrics are used with permission of the copyright holder, except for those lyrics which are in the public domain.

Prologue

Your enemies can kill you; they can kill your friends and they can kill your joie de vivre. But, only the people you love and the people who love you can hurt you. The beautiful blonde being held hostage thousands of miles from home learned these truths many years ago.

Of course, the man who brought her here and tied her up knew nothing of her past. He only knew, or thought he knew, that she could help him get what he wanted. No, not what he wanted; what he could not live without. It had started out as a want, but it was now a need.

For several days, he'd been trying to scare her. He knew he was good at scary, being scary is easy for a trained killer with his physique and intimidating presence. He didn't know the girl, but he knew killing her would be a bad idea. Every source he had, had made it clear that killing this particular girl could be a fatal error.

For many hours, he'd tried to break her by torturing her with loud, distortive music played through earbuds she could not remove since her hands were tied. He didn't prefer this method of getting information, but it had worked in several previous operations.

For about half an hour, he'd been aware that it wasn't working. Music torture is not an exact science, but this girl clearly wasn't responding. She not only wasn't bothered by the loud music, she seemed completely unconcerned by her current predicament.

For a few minutes, he wondered if any of his other methods of persuasion might be more effective. Three different nations had taught him various methods of persuasion, but as he looked at the impassive girl before him, he doubted if any of his methods would affect her.

Suddenly, he felt an intense pain in his ankle. He looked down, but he knew what he saw had to be a hallucination. In panic, he looked back at the beautiful blonde girl to see if she could somehow be responsible for his pain.

The pain only increased, and he died without getting an answer. The last things he saw on earth were the two beautiful eyes of a tied up blonde, who showed neither fear, nor even the slightest interest as she watched a five inch, eight eyed, eight legged creature cross the floor and kill a 240 pound mercenary.

A beautiful blonde girl caused his pain... and his death.

Part 1 – Rude Awakenings

"There be many that say, who will show us any good?
LORD, lift thou up the light of thy countenance upon us.
Thou hast put gladness in my heart,
More than in the time that their corn and their wine increased.

I will both lay me down in peace, and sleep:
For thou, LORD, only makest me dwell in safety."

Psalm 4
David

01   Bad Omens

It would be a mistake to say that I slept well, if, in fact, I even slept at all.

I woke up shaking in a cold sweat. I only believed that I'd slept at all because I could recall several nightmares. Nightmares are part of everybody's sleep sometimes. Mine became much more frequent and frightening the morning I found my two best friends murdered.

Moving to Dallas had started me on the path back to a more normal amount of nightmares. Meeting and marrying the man of my dreams had made them almost go away entirely.

I felt a cold compress on my forehead and a warm hand holding mine, so I opened my eyes. His loving, concerned look made me glad that I'd opened my eyes. The Absolutely Incredible Freak Show is almost as famous for his acting ability as he is for the fact that he's a living, breathing superhero. But if there's one thing I'm sure of about my husband, it's that love is the one thing he never has to fake.

He asked a question he's often asked. "Was it bad?"

"I've seen worse."

"Can I help?"

"You already have."

"Do you want to talk about it?"

One thing I love most about him is that he is always ready to listen and never tries to push me into talking. Most superheroes want to solve everybody's problems all the time. My Freak lets me solve my own when I can, and only flies to the rescue when I need him.

"I'm going to take a bath," I told him. "Let's talk about it over breakfast."

I went upstairs and drew a bath. As the water ran, I picked out an outfit and laid it out. Like my husband, I can act out almost any part I need to, but we had no scenes on the agenda for either of us today. Left to my own script, my favorite role, or at least one of my favorite roles, has always been the role of a confident, beautiful woman.

Less than an hour after drawing the bath, I was dressed to impress and sitting at the breakfast table. My wonderful husband complimented me on both my apparel and my appearance as he often does. I looked forward to later when he would show me his appreciation for the red and black lingerie he would compliment after our day came to an end.

He compliments me often and with enthusiasm at every opportunity. I think that has something to with how hurt he was when his previous love was murdered. Most lovers bring some baggage into a new relationship. Few lovers are lucky enough to find a lover with such pleasing baggage.

I smiled and blushed at each compliment. Smiling and blushing is part of most of the roles I play, but with my husband it's not an act. The only acting I ever have to do with him is when it falls on him to prepare a meal.

One glance at our breakfast table revealed a feast of cereal and a stack of underdone toast. As I sat, I noticed with some relief that the table also contained silverware, butter and a gallon of milk that was still sealed and still in date. I sat down and smiled at my husband appreciatively.

"The toast is perfect, Darling. It's not burnt at all."

He pretended to beam, "I can't take all the credit. You taught me every thing I know about being a gourmet chef."

As we ate, I teased him a little. He let me have my fun for several minutes before he changed the subject.

"I think," he said hesitantly, "we had planned to talk about something other than my lack of culinary skills this morning."

"We did," I answered. "Are you sure you're ready to listen. These weren't pretty."

"You said you've seen worse."

"I have, but I didn't say when. Last night was the worst I've had since Dr. Tinnin suggested it would help to share them with you."

"I can take it. But if you don't want to tell me, I won't press."

"No, I'll tell you, I dreamt about the ceiling fan again. Multiple nightmares in one night all starring the same damn ceiling fan and a poor dead body hanging from it."

This is the nightmare I most often have. Dr. Tinnin has explained it to me, using the most advanced jargon The American Psychiatric Association has developed. I'm sure he's right, but it doesn't take a genius to know a young lady who finds her best friend hanging from a ceiling fan will have dreams about it for a long time.

Freak also knows this. He asked, "Charlotte?"

I nodded, "Her body, anyway. The faces weren't always the same, but it was her body in the clothes she was wearing: fishnets, short skirt, low cut blouse with a little bit of her lace bra visible. That part seldom changes."

Freak's concerned look transformed to about as close to scared as it ever gets.

He asked, "How many times?"

I answered vaguely, "Six or seven."

"Crap! That's terrible. I guess I slept through the first ones. I'm sorry."

"Don't be sorry, Freak. It's okay. I've been known to sleep through your nightmares, too."

"I suppose so. Still, I wish I'd been able to stop you from going through that again and again. Whose faces did you see this time?"

"It was mostly the usual suspects." I replied, "Charlotte, Jenny, Vanessa, my mom and my choir teacher from secondary school, Miss Gruene."

Freak waited patiently for me to continue. I was thinking about the face I saw in the nightmare that woke me up in a cold sweat. Several random blondes have appeared in that dream, including some of Freak's friends and the occasional celebrity.

I decided while bathing not to tell Freak that the girl in my last nightmare was the girl I see every time I look in a mirror. Dr. Tinnin can help me work through this new development. My superhero husband has too many of his own issues to work through for me to burden him with this.

I stood up and started clearing the table. "I don't think I want to talk about the dreams right now. Let's clean up."

Freak, of course, accepted this without complaint. If I had known how bad my personal issues would get before I got another session with Dr. Tinnin, I would have told Freak every detail of the first nightmare I've ever had that starred April Show as the dead victim.

02   Friendly Cutthroat

"We should get to the office."

"Actually we shouldn't. Carl says for us to take the day off. He has a private meeting scheduled."

"Don't patronize me, Freak. I had a bad night. I'm still fit for duty. Whatever you told Carl to get the day off, call him back and undo it."

"Honey, I swear. I didn't tell him a thing. I didn't even talk to him at all about it. He called while you were in the bath. If you don't believe me, call him."

"He'd just lie about it."

"Maybe, but we both know he's a lousy liar. You'd know."

I knew he was right about that. I also knew he wasn't that great a liar himself. "Okay, it was his idea. I believe you. Why a day off? Why not work from home?"

"Work on what? We've pretty much wrapped up everything we have going."

"That's my point. Shouldn't we be drumming up some business? I don't really want to go back to tending bar, and I think you'd have trouble rounding up co-stars if you tried to put your revue back together. Everybody seems to be moving on in life."

"You're probably right about that."

He said it like he meant it, but I knew he didn't believe it. Nobody who calls himself The Absolutely Incredible Freak Show for several years would truly believe that anybody would ever want to do anything enough to pass up the opportunity to be a part of one of his performances. He may try to go by Franz Scholes again now, but he still has as much confidence as he's always had.

He waited long enough for me to comment on it, before he accepted that I wasn't going to comment, and continued. "Carl didn't say it, but I got the sense that he's working on something big. Jeff told me Carl referred a couple of cases out and told him to wrap up everything he was working on by the end of the week."

To say the least, I was surprised to hear that. "Why would he do that? Isn't he the one who always says that a case is a case and a client is a client?' Why would he suddenly start turning down business?"

"I don't know, but since the only way to ask him about it is to tell him that Jeff told me about it, I don't plan to ask. Carl's been running this agency for a long time. I trust him to keep running it."

My husband is Carl's partner, not his employee, but he seldom acts like it. He also tends to trust the few people he trusts completely. If Carl or Sam the Man or Larry Joe McCoy told Freak the sky is green, he would go to his grave believing the sky is green.

I wasted some time trying to convince him to be less trusting. Finally, I realized that Freak has an uncanny knack for knowing who to trust completely. If Carl thought something was brewing that would take all our resources, Freak was probably right to trust him about it.

I put on my Olivia Newton John happy face, "So, Lover, how do you want to spend our day off?"

After discussing several great ideas, some of which probably aren't legal in the Great State of Texas, we ended up accepting Jeff's invitation to play pool in his apartment's recreation room. I went upstairs and changed into the black high heels I always wear when I play pool.

My pool playing heels are a few inches higher than the ones Jeanette Lee wore in her video, 'The Black Widow's Guide to Killer Pool' from which I learned to win when I play pool. Since I'm a few inches shorter than her, I've always felt these heels evened the odds for me.

Jeff's apartment isn't very far from our house, but instead of walking, we hopped on DART's green line train. Freak pretended that choice was in deference to my shoes, but I know he just didn't want to be tempted to drop in at the office and bother The Great Detective. As an added bonus, riding the train gave us the opportunity to make out a little and garner a few disapproving glances.

At Jeff's apartment, the concierge put us on the elevator and sent us up to the rooftop game room. Jeff was waiting for us and gave me a polite side hug and then gave Freak a handshake that was far less complicated than the one Freak and Sam The Man always share, but still too fast and too detailed for me to follow.

Brian D. Eyre

I've spent most of my life around men, trying to understand how they think, what they want and why they act the way they do. Many men, including bosses, friends and patrons have told me I understand men better than any other woman on earth. That may be true, but the male handshake ritual completely baffles me.

Jeff had the table racked for cutthroat. He handed me a pool cue. "Ladies first," he said smiling.

I accepted his offer and promptly sank the three on the break. The seven was left on at the edge of a pocket so I sank it next.

"I guess I'll play the large ones."

Freak smiled, "I thought you told me it's better to be the middle ones in cutthroat?"

"I said it helps. I didn't say it was mandatory." I sank the four and lined up the nine.

Jeff looked at Freak and asked, "Why does it matter? All three players get five balls. I don't get it."

I sank the nine as Freak answered, "Don't ask me. She's the professional hustler."

I cut the six onto a side rail to end my turn before answering.

"I'm not a professional hustler. It's just a hobby. The middle gives you a slight edge because many players, particularly weekend eight ball players tend to ignore open shots at the eight out of habit."

Freak sank my six, then missed a shot at Jeff's fifteen. The cue ball ended up snookered behind his thirteen. Jeff tried a bank shot that he's not good enough to make and missed it by far less than he expected to.

"Almost!" He and Freak shouted in unison as they exchanged a high-five.

"I can't wait to see how you celebrate when you make a shot."

"Better yet, you could let me win. Then you could see how I celebrate when I win a game."

I knew Jeff was kidding. There are men whose egos need to be massaged by getting to win when they play pool with a woman. Jeff is not one of them. If he wanted to win, he could have invited us to play any number of games that I haven't spent thousands of hours learning to play.

By mid-afternoon, Jeff and Freak had each won several games. Even though I would never try to hustle my friends, a good pool player has to be just as good at missing shots by a little bit as she is at making shots. No reason not to practice both types when you have the chance.

Freak had just scattered the balls with perhaps his best break ever, sinking two balls and leaving him several good options, when his phone rang. He looked at the phone and then answered, "Hey Boss, what's up?"

My husband only calls one person boss, so I knew he was talking to Carl. Since a call from the boss might mean we were about to start earning our salaries, Jeff and I both put down our pool cues and listened to the half of the conversation we could hear,

Freak said, "Sure we are, Boss, and my friends don't call me Freak, either."

Freak was silent for awhile which either meant Carl was going into great detail about something, or being silent. Knowing Carl, I was betting on the latter. Freak's next sentence confirmed it.

"Okay, Boss. Not even you would call me to prove you can do the silent treatment on the phone even better than the girl in the AT&T commercial. What did you call to tell me? It can't be good, or you'd have just said it. Go ahead, I can take it."

The wait was much shorter this time. "I'm with April at Jeff's place. We can be there in a few minutes."

Freak getting a call from Carl is an ordinary thing. Carl doing the silent act is also pretty common. Even so, something about Freak's body language or tone of voice told me that this was not a normal call. I'm not sure what I sensed, but I know I was very scared, much more scared than I'd been when I'd woken up in a cold sweat this morning.

Part 2 – Big Trouble

"The shackles on my feet stayed in my mind
Souvenirs of fears through which I climbed
My body is shook and it could not rest
My hopes and dreams jumpin' out of my chest.

Through hell and the pit of snakes
I feel the black water on the rise."

Poppy Xander
Black Water on the Rise

03   Kept Secrets

"Would you like a tour of the staircase?"

If I expected Maurice Letot to be impressed by my offer to show him the staircase, I'd have been disappointed.

"That's not what I'm here for, Gumshoe. You forget, I have an office at the Pentagon. I've seen my share of staircases, secret and otherwise. Besides, I knew about your staircase before you did."

If Letot expected me to be impressed that he knew my office was a fortress with a secret staircase before I did, he would have been disappointed. For one thing, I'm always more surprised when he doesn't know something than I am when he does. For another, Sal Perlini, the previous tenant who made all the modifications told me that the government knew about them.

"Don't count on getting away with your famous silent detective act today. I came here to find out what Perlini told you this morning, and I expect you to cooperate with me this time."

My silent detective act isn't usually an act. I learned a long time ago that you generally learn more by not talking than you ever will by talking. Today, however, it was an act. I wasn't actually trying to learn anything from Letot, but I had already decided that I wasn't going to tell him anything more about my conversation with Perlini than he already knew.

"Perlini came in. We exchanged pleasantries. He walked me down a secret staircase." The mere facts that I didn't mention that Perlini showed me the staircase years ago, and I'd had plenty of time to walk down it didn't technically mean I was lying to Letot today. The fact that I had implied that the conversation with Perlini had been pleasant possibly did.

Either way, Letot wasn't impressed. "Go on."

"I not only told you what he showed me, I offered to show it to you. If that's not cooperating, I don't know your definition of the word."

"My definition of 'cooperate' is being honest with me. If he came here to walk you down the staircase, I want to know why."

I shrugged. "Honestly Maurice, I didn't even ask him that."

"Bullshit! You're too good of a detective not to have asked him. I do not believe you. Not only would you have asked him, but for some reason you'd have convinced him to tell you. Like I said, you're too good a detective for that."

Letot has a long history of only believing me when I'm lying, which I find somewhat disturbing given how high he ranks in the Department of Homeland Security. I don't know if this one counts, though. It's true that I didn't ask, but the only reason I didn't is because Perlini told me why he showed me the staircase again before I had a chance to ask why. He also gave me several compelling reasons not to share what I learned from him with Letot.

Letot spent another 17 minutes trying to learn what I'd decided not to tell him. I managed not to tell him anything without actually lying to him, which virtually assured that he would think I was lying.

Even though I hadn't actually lied to him, I also felt pretty much like I had. My wife, Emily, often reminds me that lying is an occupational hazard in the detective business, but I still try to avoid it when possible. It's also probably not a good idea to get in the habit of lying to high ranking government agents.

Once Letot accepted that I wasn't going to say any more about Perlini's visit, he told me what he'd really come to tell me. It was disconcertingly similar to what Perlini had come to tell me. After Letot left, I helped myself to a beer from our office refrigerator.

As I drank, I tried to decide the best way to tell my business partner about the trouble we were facing. Two Deep Ellum Brewery Dallas Blondes and 47 minutes later, I still hadn't decided how to tell him, so I just called him.

I got his wife's answering machine at their home number, so I called his cell phone. On the second ring, he answered, "Hey Boss, what's up?"

"I'm not your boss, Freak. We're partners and friends."

"Sure we are, Boss, and my friends don't call me Freak, either."

I didn't bother to tell him that almost all of his friends call him Freak. I also didn't immediately tell him why I called. In fact, I didn't say anything for long enough that Freak broke the silence.

"Okay, Boss. Not even you would call me to prove you can do the silent treatment on the phone even better than the girl in the AT&T commercial. What did you call to tell me? It can't be good, or you'd have just said it. Go ahead, I can take it."

"You're right, it's not good. I'm sure you can take it. I'm just not sure I can. How soon can you meet me in the office?"

"I'm with April at Jeff's place. We can be there in a few minutes."

Jeff's apartment is only four blocks from our office. He works for Pegasus Investigations, but he doesn't actually have an office here. He mostly does field work that doesn't require an office, and he has all that he needs for that at home. I should have expected Freak and April would be there since they weren't here and they weren't at home.

Freak seemed to sense what I didn't actually say. He does that often. It's kind of scary, but this time I appreciated it. "Hey, Carl. How about if I just walk over, and we can talk about it partner to partner without any employees keeping us company?"

"That would be good." I told him, without giving even the slightest thought to the possibility that it completely and totally would not be good.

04　Commodities Broker

I put the empty beer cans in a grocery sack and took them out to the trash while I waited for Freak. At 3:26, he walked into the office like he owned the place and didn't have a care in the world. Of course, he does own the place, or at least a share of it, but he also always walks like that.

For a time, I thought he walked like that because he was spoiled. Later, I realized that the only thing spoiled about him was that he had been forced to come to terms with his own mortality at a very young age and decided to make the most of every day he was blessed enough to receive.

If he had a little more pep to his step this time in order to calm me down, it was working. I relaxed a little as he walked over to the kitchenette and opened the refrigerator, without saying a word. He glanced in for 10 seconds before grabbing another Dallas Blonde and opening it before I could tell him not to.

He walked over and set it on the desk between us as he sat in a client chair. "You do realize that I'm not in recovery, right? I don't drink because I have no desire to drink, not because I'm on a twelve step program. You don't have to throw out the empties when I come in to the office after you've had two beers."

I didn't ask him how he knew that. Instead, I reached for the beer and said, "Maybe, it's me. Maybe I'm in recovery and you're just enabling my relapse."

"You have a lovely wife who encourages you to drink. You don't need me to enable you. Besides, I know a drinking problem when I see one, you don't have one. Trust me, if you did, your friends would have already had the intervention, and some of us are really good at interventions."

He had a good point. When your friends are bouncers, dominatrices, bartenders, cops, musicians, arachnologists, attorneys, and other assorted freaks of nature, interventions can probably be quite effective.

"So, what's up, Chief? You've had enough beer to calm your nerves, and I've done enough of my calm, cool and collected act to convince you I can take whatever comes. Spill, or I'm going to have April come down and pry it out of you."

It wasn't what most men would consider a threat, but it worked on me.

"This lovely fortress that we call an office is about to come under attack."

Freak smiled, "Again? Who's going to attack it this time; the good guys or the bad guys?"

"The bad guys, Freak, the type of bad guys who fall under Maurice Letot's definition of bad guy."

Freak sat up almost an eighth of an inch straighter. "Okay, Carl, you have my attention. I'm impressed, but I'm not scared."

"Let me tell you what we're up against, then you tell me if you're scared or not. Okay?"

Freak simply nodded, but I could tell he was concerned.

"Eleven days after I moved into this office, I started getting visitors inquiring about the previous tenant, Sal Perlini. Most were former associates, hoping to continue doing business with him or at least get paid for business they'd already conducted, but others were here in, shall we say, a more official capacity."

Freak asked, "Cops?"

"Some were police, but others represented various other agencies. Obviously, when I started getting regular visits from the Department of Homeland Security, I started wondering what old Sal was really up to and why this building with all its security had fallen into my lap."

"I'm sure you did. One day, I'd love to hear all the theories you came up with."

"I'm sure you would, but since I know the truth, there is no reason to discuss the others."

"Maybe, there's no reason, but since you're the one who told me the theory that the Ku Klux Klan killed Marilyn Monroe, I might enjoy hearing them. But not now, what matters now is what did happen."

"When old Sal disappeared, one of the government agencies tracking his movements knew that he would eventually come back.

The case was eventually routed to Homeland Security. They decided to take a hand in deciding who the next tenant should be."

"And Letot chose you?"

"He claims it wasn't his choice. His story is that somebody else made that decision, but then he was assigned to keep tabs on me."

"Do you believe him?"

"Did you forget who you're talking to? Of course, I don't believe him. However, I don't have any evidence that he's lying, and I don't think it matters. As you know, his method of keeping tabs on me has involved doing me, and our agency, more favors than I can count."

"I doubt that. You can count pretty high, and you never forget a favor, but I don't need to know how many. I know you don't always tell me who helps us on what cases and I'm cool with that. What was the deal with Perlini that attracted so much high level attention? Wasn't he just a commodities broker?"

"He was, but there are commodities and there are commodities. Mr. Perlini's commodities are humans."

"Slave Trade?"

"No, not slaves, mercenaries. Perlini matches up soldiers for hire with those looking to employ them."

Freak asked, "Is that why DHS got interested, tracking which countries are hiring soldiers of fortune?"

"I think they have a handle on that, or at least I hope to high heaven that they have a handle on it. Letot's interest would be better described as that of a junkie and his dealer. Perlini represents the most dangerous and ruthless in the trade. Letot hires the ones he thinks he can control and inserts them into certain military operations as the need arises."

"And you know this how?"

"He told me about that part of his operation."

"Why do you believe him?"

"Mostly because one of the mercenaries he hired from Perlini died because of me."

"Would that be James Seaton?"

I tried not to show Freak that I was impressed that he knew that, but I don't know if I succeeded.

"Yes, and because of Perlini's connection to Seaton, and Seaton's connection to several people that Letot declined to name, our office is about to come under attack."

Freak asked another good question. "Who told you this, and why do you believe it?"

I hesitated, but no longer than it took to phrase my answer correctly. "Our enemies often tell us lies for any number of reasons. Our friends sometimes tell us lies because they think they should. But when Perlini and Letot tell the exact same story, no matter how far-fetched it may seem, I can't believe that they are both lying."

Freak asked, "And they both say mercenaries are going to attack us. Why?"

I reached for the remote control. "Mostly because of what's behind door number three. Follow me."

I walked into the smaller office and used the remote to open the secret door. Freak followed me as I walked through the door and down the stairs. As we walked, lights came on in anticipation of our progress. Even though I'd been down here before, I still found it disconcerting.

Freak showed no signs of concern, awe or any other emotion. When I reached my destination, I stopped.

From behind me, Freak whispered, "I presume this connects to the public underground some place. What makes that such a big deal?"

"It probably does, but what makes it a big deal is the wall in front of us. On the other side of that is the basement of the former Federal Reserve Building. The building itself is now a private business, but the basement is supposedly impenetrable and was once suspected of being the headquarters and training ground for almost every Secret Service agent, CIA or FBI operative, and Navy Seal who ever went rogue."

"Rogue?"

"Rogue, as in, joining the Neo-Nazis, the Communist Party, or more recently Al Qaeda."

Freak laughed. "Does anybody other than you believe that a single building has been a training ground for Nazis, Commies, and radical Islamic terrorists? Seriously, dude, it's not like those groups share a lot of common ideology."

"Actually, Freak, I'm not really buying it either. But that doesn't matter. Perlini believed it enough to create the fortress we now own. Letot, at the very least, believes it enough that he believes that some of Perlini's former clients believe it."

"Okay, boss what does that mean to us?"

"It may mean that our office could be ground zero for Al Queda's next attack or it may mean that Letot is trying to use Perlini's secret staircase to scare us out of our own office."

I started back up the staircase and Freak followed wordlessly. As I closed the staircase door, I caught Freak's eye, "Nothing to say, Partner?"

"Just one question: which one is our friend, Perlini or Letot?"

"That's probably the right question. If I ever get it answered, you'll be the first one I tell."

It was a figure of speech, not a promise. When I said it, I had no idea that he was going to have the answer to that question before I did. I also had no idea how important that answer was going to be.

05   Sincere Apology

Once we were back in the office, we reconvened at the conference table by the kitchenette. I took another beer from the fridge and looked at Freak. "Letot's suggestion is that we sell the place to a shadow company that he will create. He says his office will defend it until the threat has been addressed, then sell it back to us."

"How much did he offer?"

Several people have suggested over the years that Freak doesn't have a head for business. Apparently, I don't either. "I didn't ask."

Freak smiled, "Because you don't plan to sell. That explains why you wanted to talk about this only with me. What if I tell you that I'd rather sell it than fight a bunch of mercenaries?"

The idea that my crazy, virtually invincible business partner might be even slightly interested in cutting bait and running from the fight had not even occurred to me.

I'd spent a long time thinking about how much I was willing to risk to fight for my right to office in the fortress I'd grown to know and love. In all that time, I'd never considered that Freak wouldn't want to fight by my side.

"Dude, I'm kidding; I love this office more than you do. You can sell your share to the CIA or the Gestapo or the KKK if you want to, but I'll still be coming in every day and defending my small corner of it."

"That's what I expected you to say. My plan was to talk you out of it."

"Right, boss. You were so worried about how to talk me out of it that you didn't even ask how much money you could tell me we were making. It's no wonder you don't lie often, you suck at it."

"Maybe I suck at it because I don't do it often enough. If we both survive the attack, maybe I'll try to lie more often. In the meantime, we need to try to survive the attacks. Letot must have suspected that we weren't going to sell, so he made some suggestions."

Freak laughed. "I just bet he did. Were any of them more helpful than selling the place to his shadow company?"

I honestly didn't have an answer to the question, but I shared all of Letot's suggestions with Freak. We also discussed our ideas. Our conversation was interrupted at 6:17 by a call on my cell phone. I looked down and saw that it was Letot.

It was after hours, and it wasn't the office phone, so I answered, "Hello."

Letot sounded more tense than I've ever heard him sound, "If you are not alone, get yourself alone. If you have to call me back then do so, but make it soon."

I lowered the phone, making sure the face pointed away from Freak. I stood and said, "I need to take this call in my office. Don't go anywhere, I'll be right back."

As I closed my office door behind me, I said "Okay, I'm alone. What's up?"

"Mrs. Scholes has been kidnapped."

It took me almost a full second to realize that Mrs. Scholes is Freak's wife, April. "How? Why?" I realized I was babbling, so I shut up.

"Obviously, I'm very sorry."

"Sorry, why are you sorry, you didn't kidnap her, did you?"

"No Carl, we didn't do it. We were supposed to prevent it, and we failed. Three of our agents were assigned to protect her. The one who survived was able to let us know what happened. I can give you the details if you want, but I hope you don't."

I took a deep breath. I followed it up with several other deep breaths. I needed to calm my nerves. I was mad at whoever kidnapped April. I was mad at myself for not thinking about the possibility that mercenaries might use kidnapping as a tool. Mostly, though, I was mad at Letot.

I yelled into the phone, "You son of a bitch!"

"Carl, you have every right to be mad at me. I'm sorry, but we have a situation we need to address. The agency has suggested to me that we remove you from the office and proceed with our own defense plan."

"The agency can go screw, Letot! If the agency had let me know we were dealing with kidnappers, we might have had competent people guarding her."

"Regarding your first point, that's exactly what I told them. Regarding, your second point, I apologize in all sincerity. I'd like to meet with you and Freak together to apologize again as quickly as possible."

"Okay, we're both in the office, how soon can you get here?"

"Five minutes. Do you plan to tell Freak before I get there? Or do you want me to tell him?"

"I'll tell him."

I could hear Letot's sigh, "Thank you, God!"

He hung up before I could tell him that my friends don't call me God. That was probably a good thing, since at the moment I felt like an idiot. While I was trying to figure out how to keep our office, I'd let one of my best friends get kidnapped.

Now, I had less than four minutes to tell Freak what had happened, so he wouldn't have to hear it from Letot. I put my phone back in my pocket and walked back to the table where Freak was sitting. It didn't surprise me that he already knew something bad had happened. He often does that.

He said, "It's bad, how bad?"

"Very bad, they've kidnapped April. Letot is on his way here to tell us how it happened."

Freak handled the news much better than I expected. He clinched his fists twice as he stood up. He walked over to the refrigerator and pulled out another Dallas Blonde. When he got back to the table he put it in front of me.

"Drink it."

"Okay, why?"

"Because I know you don't drink during combat. As soon as Letot leaves, the war is on. They took a prisoner, so I'm going to be taking prisoners. I hope for their sake they treat April better than I treat any prisoners I take."

I noted his choice of pronoun, but declined to comment on it. I could imagine what he and his friends could do to a prisoner if they so chose.

The right question wasn't what they could do to a prisoner; the right question was who should be the prisoner. I was saved from asking it, by the arrival of Letot. I let him in and the three of us sat at the conference table.

Letot said, "I can't tell you how sorry I am. I thought our people had it under control, but I was wrong."

Freak answered quickly, "You can apologize and tell us how it happened after I get her back. All I want to know is who took her and where she is."

"We don't know where she is, and I'm not at liberty to tell you who took her. My official assignment at the moment is to convince you to vacate this office."

"Why would we do that?" Freak asked.

"The kidnappers plan to trade April for access to the damn staircase. If you don't have access to it, they can't use her to force you to let them."

"If we let them in, then they won't need her for that, either."

"But we can't let you do that. It's a matter of national security.

Freak and Letot argued about what who could and couldn't do for 36 minutes. I mostly listened and nursed the beer that Freak had delivered to me. When I finished the Dallas Blonde, they were still arguing, and no closer to reaching an agreement.

I stood up and walked to my office. I took my Victor .22 out of a desk drawer. I'm not a great shot, but it has a laser scope attachment that makes even me pretty accurate. I was pretty sure I wouldn't need the scope for this task. I left the scope in the drawer, and tucked the Victor in my belt behind my back.

When I walked back, Letot asked, "Are we boring you, Mr. Jennings?"

"Actually, you are. I'm going to talk, now. Freak, he won't tell us who took her, because his boss won't let him, and he's nothing more than a sniveling lackey."

"Hey, that's…"

I looked at Letot with the hard look I'd learned from Detective Woodbury so many years ago. I must have learned it well, because Letot stopped in mid-sentence.

"I said I'm going to talk now, and I meant it. I presume the people who you have guarding the other potential victims are on high alert?"

Letot nodded affirmatively.

"Good, I see no reason for them to need multiple hostages, but we are talking about ruthless mercenaries. You want this office, and they want this office. They have April as a hostage, and I have the staircase as a hostage. Here are my demands. You will provide us with safe houses in several different states. You will not ask me or try to find out who we stash in which one."

"I can't do that."

"You can and you will. If you don't, I will invite the person who calls about April to come over, and I will give him the keys, the remote and a guided tour."

"You wouldn't do that."

"Try me. April is not going to die because you and your department can't protect one young lady from kidnappers that you knew were coming."

"I am here with the official authority to evict you right now if you don't agree to cooperate! Do you understand that?"

"I understand and I'm not surprised. You Washington nitwits have always placed too high a value on official authority. That's why the Branch Davidian situation became such a mess. I wish I was at least a little bit surprised that you haven't learned a single lesson since then, but I'm not."

I reached behind me, and pulled out the Victor. I pointed it at Letot and once again gave him the Woodbury stare. Letot did not react, so maybe I still need more practice with the vaunted Woodbury stare.

"Now, you will get your ass and your official authority out of our office. You can call me when you're ready to agree to my terms. When this is all over, I'll let April decide if we ever let you back in."

"And if April is no longer around to decide?"

I looked at Freak as I spoke to Letot, "Then you probably won't be around to wait for the invitation."

Letot obviously tried not to glance at Freak, but he couldn't help himself. Freak never needed to practice the stare. It comes as naturally to him as breathing air and drinking water.

Letot collected himself and turned back to me.

"And if instead of leaving now, I choose to call the agency and report that you have decided not to cooperate?"

"I either shoot you in the forehead, or we knock you out, lock you in the staircase and turn you over to the mercenaries when we give it to them."

"You wouldn't do that."

I smiled, "Try me."

He returned the smile, "You wouldn't, but I'll leave any way. Your plan sounds better to me than my boss's plan."

At the door, he turned, "It is fortunate for both of us that I am neither a sniveling lackey nor easily insulted."

He turned to Freak and smiled, "I adore April almost as much as you do. We'll get her back."

Freak smiled, "No, you don't, but *yes*, I will."

Freak sounded confident. Freak always sounds confident, even when he's dead wrong. I hoped with all my heart that this wasn't one of those times when he was dead wrong.

06　Crossed Fingers

"Well, we can scratch threatening a high-ranking Federal Official off our bucket lists."

"I can, Freak. You just sat there smiling as you enjoyed the show."

Freak gave me his petulant look. "I wasn't enjoying the show; I was smiling in a threatening way. Now what do we do?"

It was a good question, and I actually had an answer. "I call Letot and get a list of who his people are guarding. You round up everybody who you think is willing to go to war with us and let them know what's going on. Then, we compare lists and make sure we don't leave anybody in danger."

"How does this help me get April back?"

I noted again his choice of pronoun, but chose not to comment on it. Instead I answered, "It doesn't, but we have to get this part handled before we take her back. Otherwise, they'll just take somebody else."

"How do you know they won't take another, anyway?"

"They might. If they do, we'll know more about how to deal with them. Plus we'll know that they are more ruthless than smart. So far, I know they're ruthless, but I don't know if they're smart. I think they're smart, so I don't think they'll take anybody else."

"I don't understand."

"Hostages are like poker chips. You only need one to place a bet. If you need to place twenty bets, maybe you need twenty. These guys only have one bet to place, so they only need one hostage. If they kidnapped the entire country, we'd make them release all but one of them before we let them have the pot."

"Okay, I get that. I'm assembling an army in case they aren't smart."

"Perhaps, but at some point, we're going to have to take April back; an army will be helpful regardless of whether they're smart or aren't."

"What if they take several, so they can send out bodies one at a time to impress us?"

"Would you be impressed?"

"No, I'd be pissed."

"And are you pretty cooperative when you're pissed."

"Hell no, but they don't know me."

"They know me. I'm not exactly known for being cooperative when I'm mad, either."

"Trudat, Dude. You're not all that cooperative when you aren't pissed. I get it, now. I'm going to call Sam The Man and start putting together our army."

Freak stood up, and headed toward his office.

"Good luck with Letot. He might be a little mad about you threatening him at gunpoint, and we'll probably need his help with this."

"I'll handle Letot."

"Anybody you want to call yourself, or am I in charge of assembling the army?"

"I suppose I should call Blake and Emily, you can have everybody else."

"Emily? I had her listed as someone for our soldiers to guard, not one of our soldiers. No offense, but I'm kind of surprised they targeted April first instead of her."

"The way I see it, everybody who might be a target, might as well be a soldier. We don't know if they targeted April first, or if they found her first. My guess is that they targeted her because she's an employee of Pegasus Investigations. That makes her part of the enemy army and fair game."

"I thought we were dealing with ruthless mercenaries."

"We are, but even soldiers of fortune know the rules of combat. It doesn't mean they won't break the rules, but they have no reason to break them if they don't have to."

Freak shook his head. "Either that or they think that as an employee, she can get them in that staircase herself."

"Possibly, but I doubt it."

"But if they do think that, then they'll ask her to let them in; she won't be able to let them; then they'll torture her until they finally believe her and then kill her."

"I don't think so. I think they know I'm the only one with access. Perlini and Letot both know I never share confidential information without a good reason. Putting friends in danger would certainly not be considered a good reason."

Freak looked worried, as worried as I'd ever seen him look.

"Freak, relax. Their next move is to call me and ask me to exchange her for access to the staircase. We need to be preparing for that, not worrying about April. They will treat her kindly until they find out that we won't make the deal."

"So why don't we just make the deal?"

"We will if it makes sense to do it when the time comes."

"Okay, I'm going to go assemble an army."

He left and I turned to the computer to update the case notes, and maybe, put off making two phone calls I really didn't know how to make. I was saved the trouble of making the first call when the phone rang 4 minutes after I started typing.

I answered, "Pegasus Investigation, the premiere agency in the southwest."

"Carl, it's Letot. We need to talk. Is this a good time?"

"About what? Arresting me for threatening a federal official or granting my demands."

He hesitated longer than I'd ever heard him hesitate. After 45 seconds, he replied, "Neither, and both. I'm not telling anybody about the conversation in your office, but I do want to do everything you suggested."

"Everything?"

"I want to put everybody who needs to be in a safe house in a safe house. I also want you to control who ends up where, not me or the agency."

"Because I have a gun, or because you agree with me that your people would screw it up?"

"Because, at the moment I don't know for sure who my people are. You and your crazy menagerie may be the only people I can trust right now."

I laughed. "Do you really expect me to believe that? Why would I not think you're trying to trick me into cooperating with you so you can advance your career by blowing up my office to defeat the radical insurgents."

Brian D. Eyre

"You do realize that you read too much left wing propaganda, don't you?"

"I accept it as a distinct probability. I also probably read too much right wing propaganda and too much propaganda from people who are too far out there to even know which wing they might fit on if they could ever decide on a wing to land on. Is that even slightly relevant to our current discussion?"

Letot sighed, "Probably not, but we need to help each other on this, Carl."

"Tell me why."

"Have I ever lied to you, Carl?"

"Yes."

"I mean about anything you had a right to know about?"

"Yes."

"No, I mean about anything that might put you or your friends in danger?"

"Yes."

He sighed, "I mean about anything like that, that you didn't know I was lying about?"

"No, I guess not. Is this now suddenly relevant?"

"Yes it is, because if I can get you to believe me, now, we will quit being cautiously cooperating potential adversaries, and become allies. Can you do that, Carl?"

"Maybe, why should I?"

"Three reasons; one is that I've never once misled you in a manner that led to your disadvantage. A second is that both of our lives and livelihoods may depend on it."

He stopped before the third reason, so I waited for it. I heard him breathe deeply over the phone for exactly 37 seconds, before I asked, "and the third?"

He answered quickly, "Because the security of the United States of America might depend on it, damn it!"

I doubted very much that Maurice was right about that. However, I was as certain as a person blessed with my healthy degree of cynicism can be that he wasn't lying about it.

We spent another 43 minutes discussing who was most at risk and least at risk, and how to minimize the risks. I wasn't sure if we

28

were cautiously cooperating or genuine allies, but I was pretty sure it didn't matter. I needed Letot's help to keep my loved ones safe, and he needed my help to keep the terrorists from taking over my office.

The call ended with us on much better terms than we'd been on while I was pointing a gun at him. It's possible that we were on better terms than ever before.

As soon as I finished updating the case notes, I called Emily. She answered on the second ring, "Escamillo, my love, I'm so glad you called. I was just about to call you."

I don't know if Emily loves me because I'm a detective or if she reads detective novels because she loves me, but she's been calling me 'Escamillo' almost since we started dating.

I asked, "Why?"

"You're probably going to laugh, but I think I'm being followed."

"Ironically, that's why I called. You are being followed by the Department of Homeland Security."

"You're kidding, right? I'm an accountant, not a terrorist. Why would they be following me?"

"It's a long story, but I don't have time to tell it all. The headline is bad guys want your husband to give them something and DHS thinks they might try to use you to get me to do it."

"Bad guys? What kind of bad guys?"

"International terrorists: DHS pretty much specializes in that type. I'm working on finding you a safe house. Can you take some time off work, now?"

One thing I've always loved about Emily is how well she focuses when she should; no hysterics, no excess questions, no frivolities.

"I shouldn't career-wise, but I can if it's that important. What should I tell Bob?"

Bob used to be Emily's boyfriend, and is still her friend and mine, but he is also now her boss. She'd probably have been his boss, but she's much less ambitious now that she's married to a successful private eye than she was when we met. Her question was a valid question, and I didn't have a good answer.

"I'll get back to you on that. In the meantime, drive carefully and make sure the white Tahoe behind you is able to stay behind you."

"How did you know it's a Tahoe?"

"I'm a detective."

"Of course, you are. I withdraw the question. I presume you aren't going to tell me what they want from you?"

"I am not."

"Promise me you won't give it to them. Anything they want that DHS doesn't want them to have, has to be something I don't want them to have, either."

I thought about April, and Freak's fears about what they might be doing to her. I also thought about Emily winding up in the hands of those same ruthless mercenaries. I also thought about how much I value promises, and how well Emily knows that about me, and how a promise like that would comfort her. I put one hand behind my back and crossed my fingers like a six year old child would do before telling a lie.

"I promise, my darling."

07   Sheriff's Office

Since Freak was handling everybody other than Blake and Emily, I decided to walk to Blake's office and talk to him in person about it. I called his admin, Ana Marie, to make sure he was in, then walked the six blocks to his office.

Blake's door was open, and Ana Marie waved me in when I walked into the lobby at 8:13 a.m. I thanked her as I entered his office. He was at his computer typing. He glanced my way and nodded, but kept typing.

I tried to smile as I sat down. "I'd like to report a missing person."

Blake stopped typing and looked directly at me. "Oh Shit! You're not kidding, are you."

I started to ask him if that was the sort of thing people often kid about, but decided against it. In the years I'd known Blake, we'd probably joked with each other about more politically incorrect subjects than Daniel Tosh and Chris Rock combined. Instead, I shook my head.

"No, I'm not kidding. April's been kidnapped. Letot's people saw it happen, but they couldn't prevent it. Two of them were killed in the process."

"Letot? Jesus Christ, Man! What are y'all involved in?"

I might have called him out for focusing on Letot's involvement instead of April's kidnapping, but I understood it. As the de facto manager of Dallas County's Missing Persons Department, Blake had been a part of more kidnapping cases than Pegasus Investigations has had cases.

Letot, on the other hand, was a high ranking official with the Department of Homeland Security. Like the FBI and the CIA, if Letot's agency gets involved in a case, it usually means that Blake's department is removed from it.

"Apparently, the bad guys want my office."

"There are many, many bad guys. Which specific bad guys want your office?"

"Letot wouldn't specifically say, but he implied that we're talking about a team of somewhere between five and five hundred international mercenaries."

"If that's who kidnapped April, maybe you should just give them the office. You can always get another one. It's not like you're still a struggling little agency barely paying the bills."

"We could, but Letot doesn't want them to have it. Still that is one option Freak and I are considering."

"What are the others?"

"Well, we've only worked out one other plan. We seem to have decided on it before we got to any of the others."

Blake waited for me to continue, but realized after forty seconds that I wasn't continuing unbidden.

"Well, tell me about the option you're going to take."

I nodded, stood up, and walked over to close the door of his office. When I turned to walk back, I noticed from the look on his face that he completely understood what it meant that I had closed the door.

As I sat down this time, I tried to smile again. This time, I'm pretty certain I succeeded. "We're going to put together an army, take April back, and kill the people who took her."

"I knew you were going to say that. You realize that if I endorse that plan, it could be a career ending move, right?"

"Of course, why do you think I closed the door?"

"I was hoping it was so that Ana Marie wouldn't hear it and laugh out loud. You do realize that you only have a handful of people working for your agency. One has already been taken, and only one of the others was ever in the military. Do you really think you can assemble an army that can survive a battle with an unknown number of soldiers of fortune?"

"Of course we do. Why else would we have chosen this option?"

"I don't know. Freak sometimes forgets that he's mortal, so I could see him suggesting it, but I don't know why you would agree to it."

"For the record, he didn't suggest it, I did. Remember when Freak decided to let a psychotic killer shoot him in broad daylight, and I agreed to let him do it?"

"Well, I remember that it happened. If I recall, you had the good sense at the time not to tell me about that plan until it was over. Why are you telling me about this crazy plan in advance?"

"How long have we been friends?"

He didn't answer immediately, but I knew he wasn't trying to count the years. He was grasping the logic of the question and realizing that it was not rhetorical. If we lived long enough, I might one day tease him for how long it took him to put it together, but the truth was that he figured it out faster than Freak and I did.

"Jade! You think that when y'all get April back, they'll go after Jade."

I noted that he said 'when' not 'if,' but I chose not to mention it. I also noted that he said 'y'all' instead of 'we'. That demanded mention.

"Blake, we need to protect Jade, but we also need you to join our army. You have more experience with this kind of thing than everybody at Pegasus combined. You have to join."

"Carl, you know I'll do what I can, but I can only do so much. Even if I talk my boss into letting me work on it, you know as well as I do that if any Federal Agency is involved, we get benched before the referee throws up the opening tip."

"What if the feds tell your boss to make this case your main priority?"

"How would that happen?"

"Letot needs my help guarding that office almost as much as I need your help rescuing April and protecting Jade, Emily and the others."

"Seriously, you think you can talk Letot into making that call?"

"If he won't, then I know our army doesn't just have to defeat a bunch of mercenaries."

"What do you mean?"

"If Letot can't or won't tell your boss to put you on this case, then either he has betrayed me, or his bosses have betrayed him.

Either way, that will mean we have to defend that office against a few mercenaries and the entire Armed Forces of the United States of America."

"You do realize you're talking about treason, right?"

"Maybe, I've also read my history books. The founding fathers had a different word for it. If it comes to that, I'm pretty sure Larry Joe will use the phrase 'civil disobedience' at my trial.

"I'm sure he will. He'll also use a lot of other words and phrases that don't actually apply. I hope for Emily's sake that he can convince a jury that some of them do. He usually can. Why don't you just let Letot's department do its job?"

I let the look on my face be my answer

"It's been over a decade since 9/11 and there's not been a repeat. I know how cynical and distrustful you are, but it is possible that the Department of Homeland Security actually knows how to secure the homeland. Have you given any thought to that possibility, Mr. Conspiracy?"

"Not much," I admitted without mentioning that my old boss was the one people called Mr. Conspiracy. "I promise that I'll give it all the consideration it deserves after this is over. At the moment, I'm thinking about the fact that the Department of Homeland Security knew that somebody might want to kidnap April, assigned three agents to keep it from happening, and she got kidnapped the first time she and Freak weren't together. You'll have to forgive me if I'm not quite ready to turn everything over to them."

"Okay, I get it. Any other details about the kidnapping you want to share?"

"Not really, but I am here to file a report, so I guess I don't have much choice." I pointed to his computer. "Why don't you create this Missing Persons case and give me the case number, so I can give it to Letot? After Letot convinces your boss that you need to handle the case, you can follow up with me to get all the details."

He turned to his computer and I waited patiently. After he gave me a case number, I left his office to walk back to my office. On the way, I considered possible ways to convince Letot to exert his influence to get the Dallas County's Sherriff's office to assign Blake exclusively to case number 513245422.

On the walk back to the office, I came up with twenty-three ways to approach Letot. I wouldn't say the time was wasted, since I needed to get back to the office, anyway, but my brain would have been used just as productively if I'd spent the time trying to come up with ways to help Ron Washington get the Rangers back to the World Series.

08   Big Brother

As I entered the office, the phone was ringing. I answered as I always do during business hours, "Pegasus Investigations."

Letot asked, "Is it safe to assume that you filed the missing person's report on April?"

"It's never safe to assume anything, but, yes, I did. Why do you ask?"

"In your shoes, I might have asked me if that was a good idea first, but it doesn't matter. Is Blake going to be the alpha dog on the case?"

"I'm not sure if that's the phrase I'd use in your shoes, but that's certainly what I'm hoping. We're thinking some of that may depend on you and your people."

"My people? Why would we be involved in a county decision like that?"

I didn't answer immediately. I was still trying to decide if Letot was trying to pull my leg, or was completely delusional when Letot finally spoke.

"Okay, I see. Blake's afraid we might take over and push him aside. That won't happen. I want him on this as bad as you do. Do I need to make a call to let his bosses know how the Department of Homeland Security feels about the importance of Blake being in charge of this case?"

"That would help. Do you need the case number?"

Letot laughed. "No, I'll make the call. I'm pretty sure I knew the case number before you did."

I doubted that, but I couldn't be sure it wasn't true, and I was sure there was no reason to debate it. Instead, I thanked him and changed the subject, "Anything new from the bad guys?"

"Nothing unexpected, they are keeping your office under 24/7 surveillance, but as far as we can tell, it's always one operative at a time. They also aren't making much effort to keep that surveillance clandestine."

That didn't surprise me. "They know the building almost as well as we do; that's why they took a hostage. They know a paramilitary strike is unlikely to succeed."

"Don't get too cocky, Mr. Jennings. These guys aren't paramilitary; they're the real deal. Stronger fortresses than yours have been taken down. I know you pay enough attention to these things to know that."

He almost never calls me by my real name, let alone my last name. If I cared, I might have wondered why he did this time, but I was more interested in his tacit acknowledgement that the fortress in question was, in fact, mine. I found it interesting, but not worthy of comment.

"Of course, but unless you misled me, their goal isn't to take down the fortress, their goal is to gain access to it. It's a little hard to occupy a fortress after you destroy it."

Letot didn't sound impressed. "You may be right, but I wouldn't count on it."

"I won't. I never count on anything I learn from a government official. Do you have safe houses arranged?"

"I'm getting there. I also have a suggestion. I know I promised that you could deploy them at your discretion, but I'd like to suggest that you bring Emily to the one I'm setting up in the greater D.C. area."

I thought about that. I'd been pretty mad when I insisted on excluding him from the process. I'd calmed down since then, and it appeared that we were working together now. So, I didn't see any reason why I couldn't let him know where Emily was stashed.

With that in mind, I asked, "Why?"

"Because if this thing drags on, and we both know it might, you'll want to visit with her. If she's here, I can justify using department funds to fly you up here as a legitimate expense related to a case that directly relates to national security, and therefore is not likely to be subject to any expansive audits over expenses."

I would have thought all Department of Homeland Security cases met that criteria, but I was so pleased to learn that somebody in D.C. was actually monitoring how they spent our tax dollars that I decided not to comment on it.

"That makes sense to me, Letot. I'm fine with it. Speaking of this thing dragging on, do you have any suggestions how I hide Emily in a safe house in D.C. for however long it takes, and still leave her with a chance to continue her career with America's leading retailer?"

Letot laughed, "I'm not sure she actually works for America's leading retailer, but if you love her enough to call it that, I won't argue with you about it. And yes, we can sequester her without hurting her career. Employment rights in this country are pretty straightforward. While she is hanging out in a beautiful Capitol area safe house, do you think she would prefer to continue working online or simply have some time off for herself?"

"I'm pretty sure she'd like to keep working if that's really possible, but I should probably ask her."

"Yes, you should, my friend. You should also ask her if she'd prefer to have been called into military service or merely been quarantined because she's been exposed to an epidemic contagious disease."

The thought that a government employee was telling me point blank that either fiction could be accomplished with no trouble did very little to disabuse me of any of the conspiracy theories that my old boss had convinced me were plausible. Again, I decided that was not worthy of comment.

"Okay, I'll ask her. How soon will the safe house be ready?"

Letot laughed again, "I notice that you say 'house' in the singular. It restores my faith in the strength of your marriage that for at least one moment you are thinking only of your lovely wife's safety. Actually, all of the safe houses are ready. Tomorrow morning you will receive a Federal Express package with their addresses and keys. Normally we escort our guests, but you wanted complete control, so I'll have to assume you'll be able to get the guests to their homes."

"Of course I can, but I also assume the people you have protecting them also know how to tail us while we situate them."

"I would hope so. I have a plan for that, also. Get anybody you're ready to move to a safe house to your office. Text me when you're ready, and I'll call off the protection. Then you can take them. My bosses would never approve a plan like this, but I'm confident you can get your people protected as well as mine can. Does that work for you?"

"I'll need to think about it, but it sounds okay on the surface."

After I hung up, I called Emily to find out if she'd rather join the army or be exposed to West Nile virus. Her voice mail answered, and I decided that wasn't really the type of question that should be left on a J.C. Penney accounting supervisor's voice mail, so I left a professional sounding message requesting that she return my call at her earliest convenience.

Emily and I established very early in our relationship that every Tuesday night should be date night. Her career goals and my interesting, but unpredictable profession both made it hard to keep to a regular schedule, but we wanted to keep one thing constant, if possible. We hadn't always been able to do it, but just making the effort serves as a constant reminder that our relationship matters.

Her outgoing message had said she'd be in conference for most of the day. I could have called her cell phone, but I didn't want to risk hurting her career any more than I already had. Instead, I went to the Republic Garage where I park my van.

I would need it later to pick up Emily, but I needed it now, because that's where I store most of my guns. I wasn't naive enough to think my arsenal was all we would need, but I was optimistic enough to think it might help to have more of it on hand than in a van five blocks away. When I had my arsenal in order, I locked up the office and went back to pick up the van for the drive north.

With Dallas traffic being what it is, there was a better than zero chance that Emily would be getting off work by the time I got to Frisco, and I could pose the question over a fine meal and a refreshing beverage at one my relatively new hometown's finer restaurants.

It turned out that I was close enough to correct, as Emily's earliest convenience turned out to be 3:47, and I was already parked in Penney's parking lot when I answered her return call. I let her tell me about her day, which was non-stop meetings and reminded me why the corporate world was never a career option for me before I told her I was in the parking lot.

As I'd hoped, she was delighted and suggested we have an early supper at the Down Under Pub near the mall before heading to the movie theater. She suggested it, as if she'd just thought of it, but I knew better. She knows I like to be spontaneous, so even when she

Brian D. Eyre

plans out an entire night, weekend or two week cruise in advance, she always tells me about it as if the idea just occurred to her.

Of course, having it planned out doesn't necessarily make it happen according to plan. Many a date night, more than a few weekends and at least one cruise have been interrupted by my work or hers over the years. Since those interruptions, some more than others, had paid for our beautiful new home, we both try not to complain too much about it when it happens.

Since the mall is close to our new house, we decided to stop by the house first. I followed her there, which also involved following the White Tahoe that I knew would also be following her. By the time, we got home I knew that the unmarked DHS Tahoe was the only vehicle following her.

It felt good to know something related to this situation for a change. That didn't mean I wasn't going to be much happier when I had Emily tucked away in a safe house, but it did help me relax and enjoy a lovely evening with my wife. If only all soldiers could enjoy an evening like that before being plunged headlong into a battle for survival.

09   Familiar Address

Wednesday morning, as expected, FedEx delivered a package to the office. While I'd waited for the delivery, I saw a woman pacing across the street from the office. Her clothes were typical of the DHS surveillance personnel that I'd recently become accustomed to seeing skulking around..

However, she didn't have the build or the arrogant overconfidence in her stride that makes government operatives so easy to spot. As I signed for the package, I noted that the woman was filming the encounter using her cell phone. I made a mental note to remember that some government agents are capable of defying the stereotype.

I took the package to the conference table to look it over. As I expected there wasn't much in it; five sheets of paper with two keys attached to each one. No advice, no additional information, it was exactly what one would expect from DHS.

If somebody had stolen the package or if FedEx had delivered it to the wrong address, the safe houses could easily get new locks and phony residents much quicker than anybody could have done anything sinister with his or her newfound keys. Letot, and I don't see eye to eye on too many things, but I have to respect his paranoia.

I grabbed one of the papers, and looked at it. I read through the page, with the address and the directions to find the place. At first, I found the directions to be a bit anachronistic in this Google Maps and GPS decade, but I read it anyway. As I did, I realized that the directions were in fact designed to let me know the security code without sharing it with anybody who might have gained access to this package.

Granted, Duke Carlisle may have been the quarterback of the University of Texas team that beat Roger Staubach's Navy team in the 1964 Cotton Bowl, but there is almost no chance that the city of Reno, Nevada named a street after him. Even if they did, it's even less likely that the Duke Carlisle overpass exits onto Doc Lawson Boulevard.

Letot knows I use sports figures uniform numbers as a mnemonic device. He also knows that I'm one of the very few people

Brian D. Eyre

on earth who might remember the numbers of a college football player from before I was born, and a soccer player who played in a league that even most soccer fans never even cared about.

A quick glance at the rest of the addresses confirmed that Letot was indeed using the directions portion of the papers to clue me, and only me onto the security codes. I got a bit of a laugh thinking about what might have happened to the person who stole this letter and went to rural North Carolina and asked for directions to Ollie Hoops Expressway.

I looked at the keys and noticed that several brands of popular and easily picked locks were represented. I hoped the electronic security systems were a bit more sophisticated. I trusted that they would be. It would be just like Letot to put a simple lock on the door to avoid drawing attention to a place, and then back it up with an impenetrable defense system.

Come to think of it, if he had as much to do with my own fortress as I suspect and he refuses to admit, it was exactly the thing he would do. As I pondered that bit of coincidence, I was looking at the address of the safe house address Letot had promised would be near enough to being in the Beltway that he could expense my trips to see Emily.

The street name looked familiar, which is not surprising since this great nation is full of cities that are full of streets, so most street names occur over and over again, in hundred, if not thousands of cities. I had to check my case files to be sure, but I quickly confirmed that not only was the address in Baltimore familiar to me, I was familiar to it.

I had been in that house on more than one occasion. The first time I'd been there a delightful and attractive woman had given me two imported beers and told me more about her life than I'd had any right to know. She'd also helped me solve several cases.

In doing so, Ms. Courtney Remington had helped me gain favor with law enforcement personnel in several states. I was not happy to learn that her lovely three story house was actually a government safe house because it meant that at least some of the stories she told me were lies.

I was much more upset, however, because that safe house was now available for my use. I'm not an expert on safe houses, nor on all the reasons that safe houses which are in use, become available. I am aware of one reason, and I didn't want Courtney to be dead, and I most definitely didn't want Emily in a safe house which might have already been compromised once.

I wanted to talk to Letot about it, but I knew I wasn't going to believe anything he told me on the subject. Being paranoid has worked out reasonably well for Pegasus Investigations for the better part of five decades, but I didn't know how to handle it at the moment. I thought about it for three minutes before deciding to just call Letot and hear him out. I could always decide to put Emily somewhere else if I didn't like what he had to say.

Letot answered on the second ring, "Hello, Sherlock, you got the package, I presume?"

I had stopped reminding him that my friends don't call me Sherlock, or whatever else he chooses to call me, after he started saying it with me every time I do. Instead, I said, "You shouldn't have to presume. The agent you sent to confirm the transaction surely sent you the video.

He reacted as I'd hoped, "You…. what makes you think that was one of my people?"

I laughed, "Of course it was one of yours. Are you planning to deny it?"

"No, I guess there's no point to that. Even if wasn't one of mine, you won't believe it. But if it was one of mine, should I suggest that he apply with Pegasus after I fire him?

"We're not currently hiring, but I don't know if you should fire your agent for being noticed filming me. I come from a long line of paranoids, I'm not sure it's even possible to film me without me noticing. By the way, if you do fire the agent, you may suggest that she put in an application with us to hold on file for when we are hiring again."

Letot acted shocked, "She?" Acting shocked isn't really one of his strong suits.

"Yes 'she.' I saw her walking past my office before FedEx showed up. Men and women walk differently; the agent I saw filming me is not a man."

Letot laughed, probably the most joyful laugh I'd ever heard him laugh. "She's not my agent, either. Have you perused the contents of the package, yet?"

"I have. That's why I called. I have a problem with the Baltimore address."

"I knew you would. Can you meet me at DFW Airport's remote rental car lot at three o'clock today?"

"That's not the right question?"

"Always the contrarian, I usually like that about you. I'll rephrase it. Will you meet me at DFW and make sure you aren't followed?"

"I will. Are you going to pull your guys off my tail?"

"No, I'm not. I'm going to count on you to lose them. That way I'll get to show you what you need to see, and blame the department's incompetence if it ever comes to light that you saw any of it."

I noted that he said any of it, not it. That meant that he wanted me to lose his own people to show me more than one thing. I had no idea what any of it might be, but I was sure of two things.

I knew I could lose his people, and I knew everything he wanted to show me was going to be ugly. I would soon learn that I was only half right.

10   Old Friend

Having always tried, as much as can be expected from a patriotic citizen who has read the Constitution, to be allied with the Federal Government, I had no idea how easy or difficult it might be to lose a Department of Homeland Security tail.

I also wasn't sure how many agents might be involved, so I left for the airport at 1:37. Before I left I placed a call to my business partner. He seemed surprised that I was leaving town. Once he got over that, I felt confident he would convince the amazing traveling companion I was seeking to enlist.

I drove south to the intersection of I-20 and Spur 408, which is one of the most confusing interchanges in the area. I deliberately got in the wrong lane to go west, and cut across two lanes at the last second. Two cars repeated that action with me. It didn't mean both were following me, but it at least let me know which two to watch.

I used variations of that move at three more opportunities, and then entered the airport from Northgate instead the typical north or south entrance. By the time, I'd cut through two apartment complexes and one gas station, I knew I hadn't been tailed. Of course, that didn't mean DHS hadn't tracked me via satellite or an electronic bug placed on my Durango.

After all, the Constitution is just a document, and I may be a danger to the security of the homeland as far as they're concerned. The feeling may also be mutual. I pulled into the remote rental site at 2:47 and parked. Letot was already there.

He walked over to my Durango. With him was the woman who'd been filming when FedEx delivered the safe house information package. That didn't really surprise me, since I hadn't believed him about her not being an agent.

It did surprise me a little when he got in the back seat and she got in the front seat. It surprised me even more when she smiled at me and said, "So, Mr. DeMille, I guess we're going to be filming a sequel. Are you ready for your close-up?"

Even knowing that she wouldn't believe me, I answered, "My friends don't call me, Mr DeMille." I didn't believe it either, but that didn't matter. I looked at her.

I'd never seen Courtney Remington, or whatever name she was currently using, dressed in anything but the most feminine of clothing until I saw her outside my office. Now, seeing her for the second time dressed in androgynous khakis and a polo shirt, I couldn't help but notice that her total femininity transcended her outfit, as it had since the first day that I met her.

She smiled as if she'd been reading my mind and glanced ever so casually toward the backseat "Our mutual friend back there thinks it's important that we deal with this situation together. Are you okay with that?"

I had an answer ready, but I didn't want to spoil my reputation for enjoying silence by just blurting it out. While I waited a suitable period of time, I considered others, but after thirty-three seconds, I answered her.

"Does it matter?"

In my many years as a detective, I've said thousands of things that I hoped would provoke a reaction that didn't. I've also said hundreds of things that got a reaction that I did not expect. I can count on one hand the things that I said not hoping for a reaction that got one like this one.

Courtney blushed, then started to cry, then held back the tears, then started to cry again. She finally got herself under control and turned to the back seat and looked at Letot.

"Get out! Go! I'll call you later."

Letot balked, "But, I'm supposed to ..." He hesitated, "I can't leave you here. It's not safe."

Courtney smiled. "I'm safe; you aren't. Go." Her smile reminded me of the smile I'd seen my friend Bobbie Jo use years ago while threatening a Vegas club owner with death by spider. At the time I knew Bobbie Jo was bluffing. This time, I suspected that Courtney wasn't.

Letot left without further comment.

Courtney put on her seatbelt loudly without saying a word. When it was fastened, she stared straight out the passenger window. As I watched her, I put on my own seatbelt wordlessly and without making a sound. When she finally spoke, she did so without turning back toward me.

"Drive."

I started the Durango and drove. I didn't ask where she wanted to go, and she didn't volunteer a destination. I drove out the south side of the airport and headed toward Arlington where the Cowboys and Rangers have adjacent stadiums. I had no reason, but I like both teams. I also learned a long time ago that when a lady says drive, I should drive.

We were westbound on Tom Landry Highway when she turned toward me. Her eyes were moist, but she wasn't crying. "How is it that you always know exactly what to do when I'm about to have a break down?"

"I don't. I've never even seen you about to have a break down. All I've ever seen you do is deal with situations that would demolish a heavy-weight fighter with grace, dignity and one of the five prettiest smiles I've ever seen. I can't take credit for your strength."

She smiled. I may have underrated her smile a little. "We need to talk, Carl. There are some things I need to tell you. Is there a quiet bar around here where I can buy you a beer or two?"

"It's 3:15 on a weekday. I'm pretty sure every bar is quiet right now. Unless, it's going to take two hours to tell me what you want to tell me, we should be fine."

She nodded her head and said nothing. I took that as carte blanche to pick any bar I could find. I was pretty sure her suggestion was driven not by an overwhelming desire to buy me a beer, but rather her desire for a glass of liquid courage of her own. Trying to keep my streak of knowing exactly what do, I chose not to share that theory with her.

I pulled into G Willikers off Pioneer Parkway. As I'd expected, the place was not crowded. I led Courtney to a small table away from the bar. When the bartender came over, she ordered a Long Island Iced Tea, and I asked for an Amstel Light.

Her drink choice confirmed my theory that we were going to have this conversation in a bar more to help her relax than to give her a chance to treat me to a beer. I easily resisted my natural urge to mention that Texas Tea is a much more relaxing concoction than the Long Island version since a little Tequila goes a long way.

Neither of us said anything until our drinks arrived. For me, that isn't unusual, but many people seem to feel uncomfortable in silence. Courtney isn't one of those people, but she did seem somewhat uncomfortable as we waited for our drinks. When our drinks arrived, she reached for hers and drank quickly. She sat the half empty glass down while the waiter handed us our menus and started to make recommendations.

"I'll have another, please."

The waiter looked at me with one eyebrow raised. I nodded, and he left with his recommendations still unspoken.

Courtney took a small drink and followed it up with two more sips. When she sat the glass down, she looked up at me.

"So, yeah, I lied to you. Sorry."

I answered honestly, "Listening to lies is part of my job description. Don't worry about it."

She smiled. "As I'm sure you've figured out, lying is part of my job description, too."

"I have, so I don't see a problem. I'm sure you had a good reason for lying, and we're still friends, and we're still working for the same side. I've been lied to before for worse reasons than yours."

She finished her first drink, and took the second from the waiter's hand as he brought it.

"Are you sure?"

"Why shouldn't I be?"

"Because the only reason we're friends is because Letot arranged for us to be friends."

I smiled, "Even if that's true, so what? The only reason I'm friends with my business partner is because a psychopath killed his girlfriend."

"I'm not saying you're lying, but I don't believe that's the only reason you guys are friends. At least, you two have a lot of things in common. Other than the fact that we're both associated with Letot, can you name one single thing that you and I have in common?"

Several things came instantly to mind, but they were all things Courtney had spent many years and a great deal of money trying to forget, so I didn't mention them. Since I couldn't think of any that I felt comfortable mentioning, I said nothing.

She filled in my silence by drinking. Not for the first time, I wondered if all detectives use alcohol to get people to talk as often as I do. As usual, I couldn't answer my own question, so I simply drank my beer.

Courtney sat her glass down, "You're probably right. It doesn't matter if we have anything in common, and even if we do, it's probably better for both of us if we don't spend too much time talking about it. The problem is I'm not sure we're on the same side this time."

I gave that idea some thought. Obviously, Courtney's relationship with Letot was much stronger than she'd ever let on. I still wasn't sure if she was actually a DHS agent, but I knew she wasn't an innocent software designer. If Letot was seriously bent on taking my office from me by force, then I wasn't on the same side with any of his agents or associates.

I stared at her until her eyes met mine, and she set her glass down. "Right now, I'm on April's side. Unless you are trying to keep me from getting her back, we're on the same side. If you do anything to prevent me from doing that, then we aren't on the same side, and there's a good chance that we are both going to die before this is over."

"April doesn't matter. I hope you get her back. I might even try to help you if I can, but she is not important."

I thought about telling her that at the moment, April was the only important thing, but I decided not to bother. Anybody with the authority it took to cower Letot the way she had, clearly had the ability to be as ruthless as necessary.

Instead I just asked, "What side are you on?"

"I'm on my own side like I always am. I'm doing whatever I can do that will be best for little Jesse Jones from the slums of Virginia Beach. I won't go back to those slums, and I won't go back to being that person."

She pronounced the word 'person' like it was a vile curse word. She knew as well as I did, that she could never go back to being that person, but I knew as well as she did that she would always be defined to some degree by what that person had been.

I changed the subject, "What about Letot? Whose side is he on?"

She finished her drink and smiled. "That, my friend, is the million dollar question. Let me know if you figure it out, will you?"

"Sure."

"Do you promise?"

I take promises seriously. Blake says it's one of my strengths. Freak says it's one of my weaknesses. They're probably both right. I finished my beer and looked directly into Courtney's eyes. She smiled as she looked at me.

Solemnly, I said, "No, I don't."

She laughed, "Of course, you don't. Get me out of here."

I paid the bill and got her out of there, thankful not to have added another tricky promise to my list, but really concerned about the frequency with which this case was forcing me to dance around them. I just hoped Freak was assembling one heck of an army.

11   Desperate Man

I was exiting from Interstate 30 onto Commerce when Letot called. I answered almost instinctively, "Pegasus Investigations."

"Where are you?" To say he sounded stressed out would be an understatement. To say I felt sorry for him would be a complete lie.

"Don't you know? Isn't keeping tabs on dangerous men like me your department's raison d'etre? Don't you have a Carl Jennings Locator app on your smart phone?"

He sighed, "Yeah, I get it. You're mad. I get it. I don't blame you and I get it. Our meeting didn't go well for several reasons. Most of them were probably my fault, and I apologize. The situation is still serious. I think we still need to cooperate on this thing."

He paused, so I said. "I haven't said anything to suggest that I'm not still going to cooperate. I don't have to accept your apology every time you screw up to be considered cooperating, do I?"

"No, I guess not. Can you meet me at your office?"

"I can if you can convince me: why my office?"

He laughed, "Partially because we both know it's still secure, but mostly because I'm parked on a meter in front of it as we speak."

That made sense. When he realized I wasn't dropping Courtney back at the airport, he would have had to decide what to do. His agents are watching my wife, so if I went home, he'd get a notification. His agents are also watching the office, but I'm not sure he'd get a report since they're in theory protecting it from assault, not the return of its rightful owner.

I told Letot, "Okay, I'm on my way." I saw no reason to let him know how long I'd be. Instead I drove the Durango to Thanksgiving Tower to park instead of the garage where I normally park. That gave me the chance to circle in on the office and get a sense of how many government employees were watching the place.

It also gave me a chance to let Letot cool his heels wondering where I was and what I was doing. I presumed Courtney had eventually let him know she wasn't meeting him back at the airport, but I couldn't be sure of that.

By the time I walked toward my office from the south side of the library, I'd seen three agents who were clearly doing surveillance on either my office or some other building in the immediate vicinity. One of them probably noticed me, but I wasn't worried about that.

It's my office, after all. I don't have to sneak in... unless I want to. I now had a better idea how hard that might be to do from the library. I also had a few secrets up my sleeve about how to get into my office without being noticed, but those wouldn't be needed until we had April back, if at all.

Letot saw me as I approached the office and got out of his Tahoe. This one was fully decked out in DHS insignia and stripes. He jumped out and met me at the stairs to the office.

"Thanks for meeting me here, Carl. I'm really grateful."

Apologetic, grateful Letot took some getting used to. I may not have been missing bossy, 'I am the government' Letot, but I definitely wasn't used to this version.

I nodded to the Tahoe. "Nice paint job, did you switch to a marked car to scare away bad guys or to make sure you didn't have to feed the parking meters?"

He shook his head. "It still bothers you that Federal Vehicles park for free? You're an amazingly consistent man, Carl. A woman you care very much about has been kidnapped; your wife is on the target list; your livelihood is being threatened, and you're pissed off because I didn't have to drop quarters into the damn parking meter. Would it make you feel better if I went downstairs and fed the thing?"

I smiled and lied to Letot, "Dad once told me that if you don't believe something always, you don't believe it at all. When a Federal Official doesn't pay for a local service, he takes money from the local citizens and gives it to Washington. Nobody who has read the Constitution can condone that activity or any policy which permits it."

In addition to carrying on the legacy of the old man who first got me into this business, I'd managed to make Letot even more uncomfortable in my presence. Not for the first time, I wondered how many of the old man's theories were heartfelt beliefs and how many were just tools in his investigative toolbox.

As usual, Letot believed my lie about whose advice I'd just repeated. "I'm sure your dad had a valid point, but right now might be a good time to believe less in the things you always believed in, and a little more in the urgency of the things that currently matter."

"By which you mean April? You said they wouldn't do anything rash until they offered me a chance to acquiesce. Has that changed?"

"No. At least if it has, I haven't heard anything to suggest it. What I have heard may be more important though. I had hoped to discuss it with you and Mrs. Remington, but that didn't work out. Now I'm not sure what will work."

He stopped and looked down at his phone before continuing. "I need to tell you some things I'm not proud of. I could ask you to never repeat them. I could even try to get you to promise not to do it, but I'm not going to do that. I take my job at DHS very seriously. I get a paycheck, and I get to park for free at your damn parking meters, but that's not why I do it."

He looked straight at me like we were filming a movie before he continued. "I do it because I'm good at it, and I love my country. I've already decided to tell you about the mistake I made. I just want you to know that if you make it public, I will be fired, possibly even arrested. Somebody else will take my place, and they might be as good at the job as I am, but they might not."

I couldn't resist, "Bravo. Edward G. Robinson would be proud of your performance."

"Mock me if you wish, but I'm serious and I've already decided to tell you, so here goes. A few years ago, I made a mistake. I got word that you were asking questions in Virginia Beach, and I could see where that investigation could lead."

"By 'got word,' you mean the agents you had keeping track of me told you what I was up to."

"Close enough, they only told me where you were, not what you were up to. I had to follow up to learn that. As you know now, my agency had a very effective operative with a connection to the case you were investigating."

"I do know that. I also know that he got killed by fire that was decidedly not friendly shortly thereafter. I knew all that. Go on."

"In the hopes of keeping you from forcing my hand on Mr. Seaton, I broke the cardinal rule of my business; actually I broke two cardinal rules. I led a civilian to an agent of another branch."

Brian D. Eyre

He looked contrite. He also looked like he had said what he planned to say. I presume I looked vaguely interested, since that's the way I've been told I always look when I'm confused. We continued looking at each other like that for 75 seconds, before I went from being confused to being enlightened.

"I guess it's a good thing I didn't tell her who it was that gave me her phone number all those years ago, isn't it?"

"It was at the time. I guess in some ways it still is. She's known for a long time that it was me. She's just been kind enough not to act on her knowledge until now."

"What makes you think she will now?"

"Damn it, Carl! You saw her tonight. I've never seen her that mad. I don't even know what I did, but it isn't going to matter. If this situation doesn't end well, she and I will both be on the hot seat, and if that happens, I'm toast."

"Then I guess you need to help me make sure it ends well, Mister Letot."

He looked contrite again. "I'm not sure there's any possible ending left that you and I would both agree classified as ending well."

My office phone rang; the number came up as unlisted. I had a good idea who it was and what agency of the Federal Government she represented, so I answered it, "Pegasus Investigations; proudly cooperating with the U.S Government since 1965."

Courtney laughed. Her laugh sounded genuine, "Wasn't your agency founded in 1959?"

"Yes, but I take the truth in advertising laws seriously."

She laughed again, "Of course, you do. Is Letot still there?"

"Yes, he is."

"Good, I'm on my way. Ask him to stay. No, scratch that. Tell him to stay!"

She hung up without waiting for an answer. Apparently, she just assumed I would do what she said. I would have thought she'd have known me better than that. She may think she can tell Letot what to do, but I'm my own man. Besides, my mentor would roll over in his grave if he thought I was kowtowing to a government agent.

12   Federal Case

I turned to Letot and lied, "Ms. Remington is on the way over. She wants me to ask you to stay."

If he realized I was lying, he didn't comment on it. He just nodded, and we waited silently for her arrival. I don't know where she'd been when she called, but she arrived in seven minutes, so she hadn't been at the hotel by the airport where I'd dropped her off earlier in the evening.

She had changed clothes, also. She entered the office wearing a gray, pinstripe skirt suit with a white blouse buttoned just high enough to be modest and black high heeled pumps. She looked much more like the Courtney I knew, but she carried about her an air of command that was new to me.

She sat down beside Letot in the other client chair and addressed him. "Letot, I have to make this work, and I'm going to make it work. You can either help me make it work, or you can go back to Washington and shuffle papers."

He didn't say anything. He also didn't make eye contact. She turned to me. "I work for the National Security Agency. Did you know that before I just told you?"

I smiled. "I still don't know it."

"Of course, you don't. Do you believe it?"

"I accept it as a working hypothesis. Does it matter?"

"Of course, it matters. I'm trying to find a way for the three of us to all get what we want, and I don't think that can happen if we don't establish some level of trust. That's why I flew down here, met up with Letot, and wore that unbelievably drab costume for two days."

"In that case, I believe it."

Courtney favored me with her top three smile. "Maybe, it would help us work this out, if we all agree on what we want. Carl, if you don't mind, why don't you go first?"

"I want April rescued and my friends kept safe. I want to keep my office, and I want to watch everybody who was involved in kidnapping April and putting my friends in danger die. It would be a nice bonus if they all died painfully and all of my friends also got to watch them die, but I'm willing to skip that part if it makes things easier."

"Sounds reasonable, I didn't hear anything in that about official apologies or restitution from the U.S. Government. Are you and McCoy saving those for later?"

I laughed. It didn't sound like a pleasant laugh to me. I hoped it didn't sound like a pleasant laugh to anybody else in the room. "If I don't get what I want, I think McCoy is likely to be the least of the problems either of your agencies has to deal with from my camp."

Letot sat up a bit straighter, "Another threat, Carl?"

Courtney turned sharply to meet his eyes. "As the woman officially in charge of this case, I'm taking Mr. Jennings comment as a promise, not as a threat. I think your agency would be well-advised to treat it in the same way."

Letot leaned back and said nothing.

Courtney continued still looking at him, "As a citizen in good standing, and a friend, I want you to know that I want what Carl wants very badly. I second what he promised; but from me you should definitely consider it to be a threat."

Letot said nothing. I said nothing. Courtney said nothing. I learned more about Letot and Courtney in that minute of silence than I'd learned in the years since I'd met them both.

 Courtney broke the silence. "Letot, please leave. I think this can still end well for all of us. I'm not mad at you, but I believe the situation now falls under my agencies' exclusive domain. I need you and your agency to accept that position. Do you? Will they?"

Letot nodded, "I do. If they won't, then you won't need to get me fired, I'll quit." He turned to me, "Is Pegasus hiring? I have an impressive resume, and I may be willing to work cheap."

He didn't expect me to answer, and I didn't disappoint him. He made his grand exit and left the stage. To her credit, Courtney waited until he was gone to clap, "He does have a flair for the dramatic, doesn't he? I wonder if I picked that up from me."

"I doubt it; he probably couldn't even walk in those heels, let alone exit stage left in them."

She laughed. "So what do we do now? DHS will be off your arse for now, and I can keep my agency calm for a hot minute, but eventually we're going to need a plan."

"I have a plan, but I need two things to get it going."

"Name them."

"First I need to get Emily someplace safe."

"I thought Letot had already provided that, he told me he had."

"Should I trust him?"

"You probably should, but that's not your nature. My house in Baltimore is probably the best option. That's why I volunteered it in the first place. Letot's people know where it is, but they know less about it than they know about this office."

She smiled at me before continuing, "Trust me, my friend, after a tour of it, you're going to want some major upgrades on this office. What's the second thing you need?"

"I need my business partner left alone while he puts together an army. I don't even know how many priors his colleagues may have, but I don't want to lose a key soldier at the wrong moment because he or she got busted for an unpaid traffic ticket."

"My department probably can't guarantee that nobody gets arrested, but call me if it happens, and I'll do what I can. I bet I'll be able to get them released faster than your lawyer can."

She smiled, "And please, do not give me names or backgrounds regarding anybody who enlists in that army who might get arrested. I do not want to know!"

"I would never tell a lady anything she didn't want to know."

"If they have to be charged, I'll take care of letting you know. Just so you know, I think I'm glad you're the one working on this. I'm sorry you and your friends are in danger, but I think, for the sake of the nation, we have the right man for the job at hand."

She stood and walked toward the door. I stood and followed her to the door to show her out and we hugged before she left.

I walked back to the desk and made several phone calls. The last call was to Freak. I expected him not to like what I wanted from him, and he didn't disappoint me. I also expected him to make it happen, and he didn't disappoint me on that count either.

Part 3 – Mean Streets

"He leadeth me in the paths of righteousness for His name's sake.
Yea, though I walk through the valley of the shadow of death,
I will fear no evil: for thou art with me;
Thy rod and thy staff, they comfort me.

Thou preparest a table before me in the presence of mine enemies:
Thou anointest my head with oil; my cup runneth over."

Psalm 23
David

13   Street Fight

"I love you, Darling," I said to the elevator door that was closing on Freak as he went downstairs to go to the office and find out what was bothering The Great Detective. Jeff had the table racked for nine-ball and handed me a cue.

"Go ahead and break. If you don't run the table, I'll start trying crazy combination shots at the nine. Maybe, I'll get lucky and win a game or two."

"You know you could win more often if you just played the table the way it lays, instead of hoping for a miracle."

"I know that's what you always tell me, and I trust your opinion when it comes to this game."

I put on my faux pouty face, "Just this game?"

He smiled, "Maybe a few other things."

"I think, I'll not ask you to list those things. A girl needs her confidence in tact to face this mean old world."

'I'll trust you on that, too. But, I don't think it's a mean old world, I think it's a beautiful world with a few mean people in it trying to mess it up for all of the beautiful people."

The most amazing thing about Jeff, and there are many amazing things about him, is that he actually believes that. The man saw action as a marine during a very brutal war and has worked in some aspect of criminal investigations almost since the day he got back, and he still believes it's a beautiful world full of beautiful people.

The only reply I could think of was, "It's no wonder you and my husband are friends, Jeff."

He smiled. It was the most enigmatic smile I'd ever seen from him. It might be the most enigmatic smile I've ever seen from anybody who has never referred to himself as The Absolutely Incredible Freak Show.

Jeff's voice was low and smooth, "I'm not friends with Freak because we both see the world as a beautiful place. I'm friends with him because he showed me that the world is a beautiful place."

I didn't have a word to say to that, and I'd completely lost interest in the pool table. I handed him my pool cue.

Brian D. Eyre

"I'm going to the library. Want to join me?"

"No, I'll hang around and practice playing nine-ball the way the table lies."

There are many better ways to practice pool than playing yourself in nine ball, and I've taught several of them to Jeff. He has a great memory, not as great as The Amazing Raymond, but good enough. I saw no reason to remind him about any of them, now.

I had my purse in hand, and was walking to the elevator, when Jeff stopped me by calling my name.

I turned, "Yes?"

"There's something I want to tell you."

"Okay"

"Freak showed me how beautiful people can be if you do your best to make them beautiful. He makes people beautiful. I try to make people beautiful."

He paused, but he didn't seem to be waiting for a reply, which was good since I didn't have one.

"You are the only person I've ever met who is even more beautiful than the world of beauty that he paints."

My blush was not the one I've perfected as an actress on the world's stage. "Are you hitting on your friend's wife?"

His blush wasn't a practiced one, either. "No! I would never. I was talking about your inner beauty."

On the elevator ride downstairs, it occurred to me that if Jeff thought complimenting a girl's inner beauty wasn't a good way to hit on her, it might explain why a good looking, smooth talking young man like him wasn't in a relationship with a good looking, beautiful on the inside young lady.

Since I didn't have any real agenda at the library other than to be right across the street from the office in case Freak needed me, I took the long way. Instead of walking East on Commerce past the Rodeo Bar where I used to work, I walked South on Field Street toward Pioneer Plaza.

Sure, it's a little touristy, but seeing the statues of the cattle drive from above on television for years is a large part of what made me decide to move here when I decided I needed to move far away. Okay, technically, it probably had more to do with the opulent and mostly serial killer free lives of J.R. Ewing's extended family than the cows.

As I crossed Jackson Street, I got the sense that I was being followed. By the time I got to Wood Street, I was certain of it. I slowly unzipped my purse and reached my hand inside to hold my 9mm Springfield. There are many reasons that somebody might be following me that wouldn't require me to shoot them, but there are also many that would. I prefer to be prepared.

I abandoned my plan and turned left on Wood to head straight toward city hall. Just before I got to Ackard, I heard a commotion behind me. I turned around and saw two men fighting. They both wore civilian clothes, but even in civilian clothes; I could tell they'd both been soldiers. Helplessly, I watched as the guy in neatly pressed khaki shorts put a snub nosed pistol to the throat of the guy in blue jeans and fired.

Blood splattered, and I pulled my pistol from my purse like I was Bonnie Parker or Belle Starr. I'm not sure who I was planning to shoot, but I was ready. I was still ready to shoot when I heard more gun shots and felt a sharp stinging sensation in the back of my neck.

I think I heard my gun and my purse hit the ground before I blacked out, but I'm not sure. I know I didn't have either with me when I woke up.

14 White Van

When I did wake up, I was disoriented. My first thought was that I was glad I'd dreamed about something that didn't include that damned ceiling fan this time. I was still trying to sort out the street fight and the shooting in last night's nightmare when I suddenly realized that it wasn't a nightmare at all.

I'd really seen an actual murder, instead of just finding the murder victims like I usually seem to do. At the very least, I'd actually witnessed a murder attempt. I saw a man get shot in the throat from point blank range. I saw no reason not to think of it as a murder. I couldn't remember anything after that except more gun shots. I figured I must have been shot, too. If so, I was probably lucky to be waking up at all.

I heard two male voices talking, so I decided to listen before I opened my eyes. I may be lucky to be waking up, but it didn't seem likely that I was going to be happy with what I was waking up to find. The longer I appeared to be asleep the more likely it might be that I would hear something that might help me know what was going on and deal with it.

I quickly realized that listening wasn't going to help. Whatever language they were speaking, it wasn't one that I'm fluent in. Since, I'm only fluent in about a half dozen dialects of one language, that didn't surprise me much. What did surprise me is that the language didn't appear to be one of the multiple languages that I had at least become reasonably acquainted with, either on church missions or as a bartender.

Reluctantly, I opened my eyes. The language instantly changed to English.

"Good morning, Sleeping Beauty. Did you sleep well?"

His voice was a deep baritone, and I still couldn't place the accent. If English was his second language, it was a distant second. I saw nothing to be gained by answering a question that was clearly rhetorical. I looked around and quickly realized I was bound to one side wall of a white van with no windows.

The two men who I'd heard talking were in the front seat. The man who spoke to me was in the driver's seat looking back in the

64

review mirror through an open panel in the steel frame wall that separated the cargo area from the front seat. I could barely see the other man at all.

"If you plan to scream for help, you should start now."

If screaming for help was likely to help, he wouldn't have suggested it. Plus, screaming loud is not one of the gifts God bestowed on me. I doubted if my loudest scream would carry much farther than his normal voice. He took his eyes off the mirror and actually turned around to look at me eyes to eyes.

"You don't want to scream?"

Of course, I wanted to scream. I also wanted to tell these sons of bitches to go to Hell. It even occurred to me to remind them that I know some powerful people. In the end, I decided none of those things were likely to help. Instead, I did what always seems to work for The Great Detective. I said nothing.

I continued saying nothing for several minutes. The men in the front seats filled the silence by talking to each other in the language I was currently thinking of as Not English. As I continued not to understand a word they said, my mind flittered, and not in a good way.

My day had started with a nightmare in which my dead body hung from a ceiling fan. That was followed immediately by an almost unprecedented complete day off. The billiard games which followed were interrupted by a phone call from an obviously distressed Carl Jennings.

That call also distressed my husband, Freak Show, who is famous for many things not the least of which is that it is almost impossible to distress him. Shortly after that, I watched a man get shot in broad daylight on the streets of Downtown Dallas. This day had turned bad a long time before I got kidnapped.

My thoughts were interrupted by the baritone voice.

"You aren't answering my questions, sweetie. Did you have to sign an agreement to use the silent act on everybody in order to get your job at Pegasus?"

"You know I work at Pegasus?" I tried to sound indignant, but in fact I was relieved.

Brian D. Eyre

"Of course, we know. Why else would we need your assistance?"

The standard issue creeper white van with no windows had given my mind several possible answers to that question, but I saw no reason to share any of those thoughts. I suspected they'd already thought of some of them, but I wasn't going to contribute to those thoughts if I could help it.

"I thought maybe you wanted a tour of Dealey Plaza, so you could hear some theories about what really happened to President Kennedy."

The man in the passenger seat laughed. It was not a pleasant laugh, but it was a laugh he clearly enjoyed. "Nobody in this shithole country who knows what happened to that Cossack freebooter is still alive to talk about it."

I suddenly realized that the accent was probably Russian. Two Russians kidnap a girl who works for the foremost authority on conspiracy theories in the Dallas-Fort Worth Metroplex, and one of the Russians refers to the United States as a shithole country and to John F. Kennedy as a Cossack freebooter.

A lot of bad things can happen to a girl who walks the streets alone. Some of them are painful, some of them are permanent. Very few of them have national or global implications.

I had a bad feeling that before this was over, I might be wishing I'd been kidnapped by a standard issue white van creeper.

Part 4 – Freakish Powers

"Release the hounds
Breathe in the sounds
Cover your ears
When the blackness nears

Cut through the seams
We'll keep it clean."

Long Sword Spectacular
"Threat Display"

15   Trained Killer

As my godfather, the famous and infamous defense attorney Larry Joe McCoy, often says 'overconfidence is pretty much my stock in trade.' I was a freshman in high school the first time he told me that. Not coincidentally, it was also the first time I needed his professional assistance to get me out of a jam that my overconfidence had caused.

I'd been sure he meant it as an insult that first time, but over the years, I've come to wonder. I don't know if that's because he's changed the way he uses it, or because I've changed the way I feel about it.

Either way, I knew from the first second I heard Carl on the phone today that I would need every bit of overconfidence I could muster. I mustered at least enough to give Carl enough confidence to threaten a high ranking Department of Homeland Security official. Now, all I had to do was to live up to my commitment to assemble an army capable of backing up his threat.

My first step was to call Jeff. I called his apartment phone, and he answered on the first ring. It took five minutes to tell him what had happened and why. It took another ten to explain what I needed him to do. In that time, he never asked any questions that weren't procedural in nature. He didn't sound scared, mad or in any way involved.

He sounded exactly the way he would sound if I asked him to come to the office and pick up a subpoena that I needed him to serve. To him, every case is just a case, even a kidnapping case. That man's ability to focus on the task and only on what the task requires should be the stuff of legends.

When I finished, he assured me he'd take care of everything and said goodbye. He was on the case and he had his marching orders. The fact that the kidnapping victim in this case had very recently been kicking his butt in a friendly game of billiards didn't matter. Neither did the fact that she was his coworker, his friend and the wife of his boss. His professionalism allowed me to chase the windmills I was about to chase without feeling guilty.

I don't actually know anything about assembling an army. I'm not even sure how many of the people I know have ever killed anybody. But, I do know some people who are capable of some impossible feats that make my inability to feel physical pain seem ordinary. Managing a freak show for three years is a great way to meet freakish people.

I also know one person who has been trained to kill by the same experts that trained our enemies in this battle. Sadly, Lamont Washington's personal enemies likely preclude him from being a valuable soldier, but I thought it might help to pick his brain a little about the process of building an army. He's helped me in the past, and his time is usually far less expensive than it is valuable.

I walked over to the street corner where he usually plies his trade and was a little surprised to see that instead of panhandling, he was selling StreetZines. Many people think that's the same as panhandling, but it is significantly different for several key reasons. Primarily, selling the newspapers is legal in downtown Dallas, whereas panhandling is not legal in the Central Business District. That may come as a surprise to those who live or work here, but it's true.

For me, the more significant difference is that you can lose your gig selling StreetZines if you get caught drinking alcohol while doing it. If Lamont had truly conquered that particular demon enough to sell the papers, my desire to talk to him for advice could change to a desire to hire him. I was definitely willing to pay Lamont for a little professional soldiering; maybe even a lot of professional soldiering.

As I approached him, I held my hand out to shake. He accepted my shake and I pulled him close enough to give him a half man hug. His breath smelled of really cheap mouth wash, which smells nothing like alcohol. I asked, "How many papers you got left?"

He's always had a sharp mind when he's sober, so I wasn't surprised when he answered without counting them, "seventeen."

I pulled out four tens and handed them to him. "I'll take them all."

He smiled and handed them to me and picked two of the tens from my hand. "I'm out of the charity business. They're a dollar apiece."

I thought about arguing, but I decided against it. When a recovering alcoholic turns down an extra twenty dollars, there's a good chance more than his pride is at stake. "Can I buy you a meal?"

"Nah, I'm flush." He waved the ten's in my face as he spoke, "But I'll join you for a meal. I know this cozy little joint in the West End where we can go."

I knew that there were no cozy restaurants in the West End that twenty bucks would cover, but I was pretty sure I knew which restaurant he was talking about, so I agreed to join him. We walked in silence, and as I'd expected he went straight to the McDonald's by the Dart West Transfer Station.

Lamont went first and ordered from the dollar menu. I saw no reason not to do the same, so I followed suit and we found a seat. As he put the straw into his courtesy cup of water, he asked, "So what's on your mind? Are you hoping to buy absolution or information today? I didn't see anybody shoot you recently, so you must just be feeling guilty about something."

I hadn't really planned out what I was going to tell Lamont. If I had, I might have answered differently, but I didn't. "They kidnapped April."

He stopped all movement and stared at me. "Okay, you're serious. You can joke about almost anything, but I know you can't joke about that. Who do I need to kill first?"

"Easy there, big fellow, I don't know who needs to be killed, but even if I did, why should you do it? I'm perfectly capable of killing, you know."

He gave me a brief glance, then returned to his food. The glance was contemptuous; I don't know if he meant it that way or not, but it was. I was co-owner of one of the Southwest's fastest growing detective agencies, and a homeless man had just mocked me with one glance.

The sad thing is he was right. I'd never killed anybody in my life. How did I know if I could do it? I'd set a guy up to die once, but I hadn't killed him. Detective Woodbury did that part. Lamont, on the other hand, had killed people. He knew he could do it, if he could stay sober.

He finished one of his burgers and looked at me again. "You probably can. You ain't no wimp or blowhard, and I know April's that important to you. I believe you can, but I think I'm supposed to do it for you."

Brian D. Eyre

"Why do you say that?"

"You know, there's lots of things can make a man lose sleep at night. You've been through some of them; and I know you've spent some sleepless nights because of them. But only two things can make a man lose sleep every night; make him cry and beg and pray and want to sleep for even a minute so bad that he's willing to die just to keep from ever being awake again."

He went back to his second burger so I could think about that. I thought about it while I ate mine. I was pretty sure I knew what he meant, but I wanted to hear it from him. Mostly, I wanted to hear it from him because I thought he wanted to tell me. I waited until he finished his burger to ask, "What are those two things?"

"I thought you'd never ask. The first one is taking another life. In my case, it was taking a whole bunch of lives that never did one damned thing wrong except having the bad luck of being born in the wrong back-ass third world country and not having any way to keep men like me from ending their sad, pathetic lives."

In the years I've known Lamont, that's the most he's told me about his service time. He told me he was in the service when he became an alcoholic, and he told me about how the alcohol had led him into a progressive series of bad decisions that had led to his dishonorable discharge.

He'd even mentioned that punching a K9 dog and shooting an MP had been the final straws. This was the first time he'd ever sounded contrite. I knew what his other reason was going to be, but I asked, anyway. "Is the second reason booze?"

He smiled. As usual, it wasn't a pretty smile., "Close, the second reason is being so drunk it's time to pass out, but you can't because every time you close your eyes, you see a kaleidoscope of innocent faces begging you not to kill them, even though you know you killed every damned one of them already."

I thought about that. Killing people had obviously had a profoundly negative impact on Lamont's life. I wouldn't think he would want to do it again.

"So what makes you think you're supposed to do my killing for me? I would think you'd want to be done with that."

He grinned. His grin didn't show any teeth. That alone made it a better look for him than his smile, but when he did it something twinkled in his eyes. "Let me tell you a story."

I nodded my assent.

"For many years, I've prayed every night for four things: a good night's sleep, forgiveness for the things I've done, the strength to get off the booze and a chance for redemption. I know God heard every one of those prayers, because that's how God is."

He looked at me as if daring me to contradict him. If there's ever an appropriate time to argue about God, and there probably isn't, this definitely wasn't one of those times. I nodded encouragingly.

"A long time ago, a man told me God never says 'no.' He only says, 'Not now.' Two weeks ago Thursday, after I said my prayers, I slept like a baby. The next day, you and April walked by and gave me a nice donation."

I had forgotten that, mostly because it was a pretty common occurrence. I tried to remember if he'd looked like he slept better the previous night, but was ashamed to admit that I hadn't really paid any attention.

Lamont continued, "I took your money to Andrew's, but they were out of Mad Dog, so I just skipped it. Even when I'm flush, I hate to overpay. "

I saw no reason to remind him that there are two other liquor stores within walking distance of Andrew's, mostly because I knew that he knew it as well as I did. Instead, I just said, "Always respected your business acumen."

He grinned, "I know you have. You once told me I'm one of the top homeless entrepreneurs in Dallas' Central Business District. I was going to put that on my business cards, but I just ain't got around to getting business cards, yet. Maybe, if I stay sober long enough, I'll get some made."

"Good to have a goal, how long do you plan to stay sober?"

"I'm supposed to say, one day at a time, but right now, I'm thinking I plan to stay sober long enough to get a shot at whoever kidnapped April. I've been sleeping like a baby since I've been sober, and I don't think killing some bastards that are really guilty of something is going to change that."

Brian D. Eyre

There were a number of things wrong with his logic, but knowing he might never have to sleep again because they killed him, I let it slide. I ate the last of my fries and watched as he finished his. I looked at him without saying anything.

As we put our trash back in the bags to throw away, he said, "Thank you for not mentioning that I might die before I get a chance to test that theory. I know you thought it, but you kept it to yourself, why?"

"It just didn't seem like the right thing to say."

"It wouldn't have been. I know you don't really believe in my God. But I believe in Him. Even at my lowest moments, I've always believed He is going to give me a chance to redeem myself. I believe this is that chance. You don't have to agree with me, but we don't need to debate it."

He said it firmly enough to make sure it was final, but it wasn't necessary. I believed this was his chance for redemption as strongly as he did. After all, only a benevolent and engaged Divine Power can cause a liquor store to be out of the world's most famous cheap wine on a warm Friday afternoon. I knew that Lamont needed to be involved, but I seriously doubted if he truly understood how expensive redemption can be.

74

16   Mistress Caroline

I was now one for one in my quixotic attempt to drum up an army of folks willing to joust at windmills that actually exist and use AK47's instead of lances when they joust. That was the good news. The better news was that my first jouster was just as well trained as the enemy. The bad news was that we didn't have any of the artillery the enemy had.

It's possible that the Great Detective's friend, Letot, or one of his real friends in law enforcement, might be willing to get us some weapons. I strongly preferred to acquire our arsenal under the bridge. I felt sure I knew somebody who could make that happen.

I seriously doubt that Mistress Caroline owes me or Pegasus Investigations any favors, but I know she thinks she does. That's usually what matters most. In addition to being my friend Rachel's boss at one of Dallas' most well-respected dungeons, she trades in various goods that the police would probably love to catch her trading, but certainly never will.

She also works long hours running those various businesses, so I had no qualms about calling her at eight o'clock in the evening. She answered on the third ring, "Hello. Is this really the Absolutely Incredible Freak Show?"

"Of course it is. Does caller ID ever lie?"

She laughed. "In my business, you'd be amazed how often it lies. Sadly, some people are still ashamed of their perfectly normal hobbies and fantasies."

Some people might argue with her about that point, but for obvious reasons, I'm not one of them. I could have mentioned that their shame is probably the reason they pay her staff to indulge them instead of finding a girlfriend, boyfriend or both to indulge in their hobby, but I saw nothing to be gained by that.

Instead, I said, "Speaking of shame, I need to talk business. Can I meet you somewhere, soon?"

"Of course, why don't you and April meet me at the dungeon when it closes around nine? If our business is private, you and I can meet in my office, and Rachel and April can play around in the other rooms. I know April has a great career with Pegasus ahead of her, but that girl could make more money in a week working for me than your entire agency makes in a year."

I doubted that, but I couldn't be sure. I tried hard to sound casual, as I said, "April is a bit indisposed at the moment. Can I just meet with you?"

She gasped. "Indeed! Okay, where are you? I'll be right there."

I'm not sure how she sensed the urgency or why she was so ready to drop everything and meet me, but I appreciated it too much to argue. "I'll be at home in about five minutes."

"It will take me longer to get there, but I'm on my way. If you need anything this second, just name it, and we'll haggle over price when I get there."

Mistress Caroline deals in so many different commodities, I was reluctant to speculate on what she thought I might need this second. "It's urgent, but it's not quite that urgent. I'll see you at my house."

The winding route I took back to the house made it take closer to ten minutes than five, but I was still there in time to be waiting when Mistress Caroline arrived. As usual, the high heeled black boots that she wore regardless of the weather made a distinctive sound as she approached the front porch.

When I let her in my front door she walked to the kitchen table. The dynamics of power are Mistress Caroline's stock in trade, but I wasn't sure if she was trying to gain power or just preferred the table to the living room. I didn't balk. I simply sat down at the table as if that had been my plan from the beginning.

She smiled, "You don't faze easily, do you?"

"I never really thought about it, but I guess not?"

"You don't lie all that well, either. But it doesn't matter. Do you wish to tell me about April being a bit indisposed at the moment, or do you prefer that I let my fertile imagination run rampant and unchecked?"

"Would you believe me if I told you she'd been kidnapped?"

"Of course, my dear boy, I almost always believe people when they tell the truth. My sources have been whispering about a private eye being kidnapped. When you mentioned that she was indisposed, I knew she was the one. I just wondered how honest you were going to be about it."

Carl often tells me that the more you know, the better prepared you are to negotiate. Mistress Caroline seemed to grasp that point well. Of course, appearing too eager can only hurt that advantage and she was the one who dropped everything to rush uptown.

"I'm going to be honest every time I think the truth will help me get her back. I am also going to lie every time I think a lie will help me get her back. And I don't believe posturing, negotiating or playing word games with you will help me get her back, so I don't plan to do any of those things."

We were looking straight at each other as I was speaking. If she had a reaction, I couldn't read it, so I continued.

"I need guns; the best, most dangerous guns that money can buy. I also need to get them without one single employee of any government agency knowing that I have them. Can you get them for me?"

"Jesus Christ! Who the Hell kidnapped her?"

"I don't know that, yet. All I know so far is that they have the types of guns I want to buy from you."

"You're probably lying about not knowing, but I don't care. You already said you were going to lie, so that's almost like telling the truth. It might surprise you to know, that I don't actually have anything like that in stock, but I'm sure I can fill the order. When do you plan to storm the castle?"

I smiled. "We're probably going to need to find the castle first, but I'd like to have an arsenal ready when we do."

"I understand. How many knights in shining armor do you have in your cavalry, and do any of them know how to operate the kind of artillery you're talking about?"

"So far, I have the staff of the agency, minus April, plus one other, and the four of us do. But, I haven't started recruiting yet. Get as many weapons as you think I can afford, and I'll find soldiers to use them, and I'll get them trained."

She smiled. "I'm sure you will, but you lied again."

"Did I?"

"Long before I became Mistress Caroline, I was a Gunnery Sergeant in the United States Marines. I not only know how to use them. I know how to train people to use them."

"Impressive resume, If that means you're volunteering, I accept. Now, I have the agency, plus two others."

"I'm not volunteering to join; I'm demanding it. I won't speak for my girls before I get a chance to talk to them, but I'm confident the rest of my staff will want to enlist as well."

"I'm sure Rachel will. She's always up for a fight, and I doubt if she'd let her husband go into battle without her, but why would the other girls want to risk their lives?"

"You're a man, so you probably will never understand how a strong woman reacts when another strong woman comes under attack. I don't say that to insult you, only to answer your question. A man, even a good man like you can never truly grasp the primordial nature of the bond that all women share when one of our own is in danger."

"I'll take your word for that, especially since I'm not even sure I understand what it means. If they wish to sign up, they'll be welcome. I'd prefer if you'd let me recruit Rachel. I think she'd be hurt if she didn't get a personal invitation."

"Probably not, but that's fine. I won't say anything to her about it."

She stood up. I knew when she said she was coming uptown that the meeting would start and finish on her terms. Mistress Caroline's need to control every aspect of her life is legendary and probably symptomatic of severe psychological issues. Her issues are not my problem, and her help is very much appreciated.

With that in mind, I simply walked her to the door and asked her to let me know when she had our arsenal. She was almost out the door when she stopped, stepped back in and closed the door behind her.

"Do you have a place to train this army?

"I hadn't really thought about it. I guess we could do it at the office."

She looked around. "The Marines don't train at the Pentagon. Your office is headquarters. I demanded to be on the team, I am not demanding this, only offering it up if you wish. We can use my dungeon as a training facility. It is well suited for the task in several ways, not the least of which is that law enforcement in the area has long been motivated to take no notice of anything that goes on there."

"That's a generous offer. Are you sure your customers won't mind? Military training can be loud."

She smiled broadly, "My customers are neither inclined, nor permitted to object to anything that occurs in that building."

I knew better than to laugh since I know Mistress Caroline never jokes about anything. Instead, I just accepted her offer and hoped that if somebody was going to die in her dungeon again, it would be somebody who deserved it.

17   Nigerian Nightmare

My army was coming together better than I had any right to have expected. Jeff, Lamont, and Mistress Caroline had all been trained by the United States Armed Forces. I had done time in ROTC, and Carl has been a detective for more than twenty years. We didn't yet have an arsenal, but I knew we soon would have.

Now, I needed to recruit the one soldier who had been trained by somebody else's armed forces. Recruit probably isn't the right word for it. Sam The Man had promised years ago that he would do anything, including kill or die, for me. It's the kind of thing good friends often say to each other after a few drinks.

Neither Osalumense nor I drink, though. He said it only because he meant it, and he's proven it time after time since then. As I walked to Deep Ellum to talk to him, I knew I was doing so more to recall a soldier from active reserve than to recruit a new soldier.

It's a bit of a miracle that Deep Ellum still exists given the number of times it's had to reinvent itself since it earned its name almost a hundred years ago. Since I first started hanging out here, very few things had remained constant. One of those was Sam The Man working the door as a bouncer at some club or another.

He's worked at more different clubs than he's had fights; partially because Deep Ellum isn't nearly as rough as it used to be (and one can make a case that it never was), but mostly because when the bouncer is seven foot tall with the body of a UFC fighter and the tribal tattoos of his home country of Nigeria, people tend to choose other locations to prove how tough they are.

Osalumense currently plies his trade at Club Dada on Elm Street. I hadn't looked to see who was playing, so I had no idea what time the show started or how early the crowds might start lining up. Regarding the former, midnight was a better guess than ten o'clock. The latter was entirely dependent on who was playing and whether or not they were the flavor of the month, week or fifteen minutes.

Either way, if Osalumense wasn't at the door yet, he wouldn't be hard to find. I knew he would be somewhere in Deep Ellum. I also know he's too large and Deep Ellum is too small for me not to be able to find him.

As I neared Twisted Root Burger Company, I heard a familiar baritone call my name. I looked that way, and saw him sitting on the patio. I jaywalked across the street. Deep Ellum isn't really a riot waiting to happen like scared suburban parents think it is, but it could become one in a hurry if the cops decided to start hassling people for crossing the street.

He was alone at a table with a glass of iced tea. We exchanged pleasantries and a fist bump series that has become so complicated over the years that I'm pretty sure we don't get it completely right every time.

He asked, "What brings you to Camelot without Queen Guinevere?"

He asked it lightly, of course, since he had no way to know that my queen had been kidnapped and that my castle was under siege. He probably expected me to remind him that I'm not King Arthur, a game we'd played many times before. Instead, I said, "Because I need you, Sir Osalumense and your fair Dame Rachel, to help me rescue Queen April from the evil Barony."

He stood up, "Do we ride now?"

"No, we don't know where she's being held. Hell, we're not even sure exactly who has her."

He sat back down, "Good, I just ordered the Western with fries and I'm starved. What do we know?"

"We do know that it's not just a crazy lunatic, or somebody hoping to collect a nice ransom. We're dealing with a well trained paramilitary force that wants to exchange April for access to something that might or might not be a threat to national security."

He sighed, "Oh, that again. You should probably get something to eat, too."

The McMeal I'd shared with Lamont seemed like a long time ago, so I walked to the counter and ordered the Bacon Bomb Burger, fries, and a root beer float. When I returned to the table and sat down, I could see in his look that he wanted desperately to hear that I'd changed my mind, and we could ride now.

"Sorry, this is just a recruiting trip. As soon we have a plan, I'll let you know it. Let's just enjoy some good food, and we can talk about the situation. We need a lot more recon before we can fight. No offense, my friend, but recon isn't really either of our strong suits."

He nodded, "I know, we've been over this before. I'd stand out like a giraffe at a cheetah convention if I tried to hang out at a Black Panther party. I'll be ready to contribute what my strengths will allow me to contribute when the time is right. My question is why the recruiting trip? You knew I didn't need to be recruited. Hyenas scavenge, rhinos charge, and Sam The Man fights at the side of the Absolutely Incredible Freak Show. These are the three unchangeable laws of the jungle. They are not open to dispute."

I smiled, "Mostly, I just wanted to hear which lame clichés from the African jungle that nobody in Africa ever uses I could get you to regale me with this time. How long has it been since you've patrolled the wilds of the African Plain?"

He laughed, "I couldn't find the African Plain if you dropped me off in the middle of it, Freak. You know that."

He waved one arm demonstratively toward Club Dada and the heart of Deep Ellum. "This close to the wilds I do patrol, you can't expect me to drop out of character."

I favored him with a courtesy smile, after which we ate in silence. Many Dallas foodies claim that Twisted Root was a better place before they expanded and opened a few stores in the suburbs. They might be right, but even if they aren't, I'm not about to debate it. I learned a long time ago that it's never a good idea to argue with a foodie.

What I do know is that being able to enjoy a big burger with three strips of bacon, fries and a root beer float any time I want is definitely on the list of good things about living within walking distance of Deep Ellum and having a condition that guarantees that I don't have to worry how well my ticker will be pumping when the AARP starts sending me letters.

We finished at about the same time, and as I'd expected, he wasn't planning to settle for my earlier evasion of his question. When his tea was refilled, he looked at me, "One more time, why are you here?"

I smiled, "Technically, I'm here because you called my name when you saw me whistling to myself as I strolled innocently down

Commerce Street. But, I was in fact ambling down the street hoping to talk to you about how to enlist Rachel."

"Yes, you hinted at needing her. Why? Are you really thinking her talents with a whip are going to come in handy?"

"Every talent may come in handy, but I know that doesn't really answer the question. Here's the thing, or should I say things. First, you're in, and we don't yet know exactly what your role is going to be. If you're at the front of the cavalry, do you really think Rachel will stay at home sewing flags while you go?"

"Of course not, she'll want to fight at my side, like we always do."

"And do you plan to tell your lovely wife, that she is not allowed to join you on the front line of this fight?"

He laughed, "Not if I want to have a place to live if I survive the conflict."

"So, the question isn't will she join, but who will recruit her?"

"Why should it matter? You're the king, I'm your Knight and she's my Dame. Either way, she'll fight at my side as I fight at your side, or she'll fight at your side as I fight at her side. Isn't your partner the one who normally frets too much about social protocol?"

I never really thought The Great Detective spent too much time fretting social protocol, but I knew it was time for me to quit fretting it.

I stared at him, "The problem is that Rachel's boss is also in the fight. Mistress Caroline plans to recruit all of her girls to join, but I asked her to let me do it. She reluctantly agreed, but I'm not sure how long she'll wait."

"Mistress Caroline volunteered for your army? Wow, I knew April has her affect on people, but I thought if anybody would be immune, I thought it would be that whip bitch!"

I didn't say anything, but I did do a double take.

He went on, "Hey, I'm not trying to disrespect my wife's boss. Rachel loves the job and that woman. I'm just suggesting that the woman is pretty good at focusing on her own self interests twenty four hours a day and seven days a week. I'm not sure why she wants to go to war. Does she even know what she's getting into?"

Brian D. Eyre

"Do any of us? I know she knows more about this type of combat than you or I do, and I welcome her help."

He looked at his watch. "If you do, I do. I learned a long time ago to trust your judgment of people better than my own. I've got to get to work. I'll recruit Rachel for you tonight. Anything I'm not supposed to tell her."

I smiled, "Of course there are things you shouldn't tell her. Fortunately, you don't happen to know any of those things, since I'm smart enough not to tell them to you."

He laughed. "There you go! Now you understand why I trust your judgment. Hey, man. I saw Spineless last night at Reno's. He could be a big help, if you can talk him into it."

"He could if I could find him, but I don't have his digits."

"I do." He reached into his pocket and pulled out his iPhone. In less than a minute he sent Spineless Spicoli's contact info over to my HTC Android, and I had a new soldier to recruit. This one might really have to be recruited, but I was willing to push hard to do so. After all, he definitely isn't called Spineless because he lacks courage.

18   Spineless Spicoli

As I walked home, I called Spicoli's cell phone number. He answered on the second ring. "Hello?"

"Is this Spineless Spicoli, the world's greatest contortionist and second greatest escape artist?"

"Freak? So great to hear from you, but I am no longer the greatest contortionist or the second greatest escape artist."

"Really? Why not? Did you retire?"

"No, even if I do retire, I won't really retire. Some crazy Chinese chick passed me as a contortionist. I swear to God, I don't even think that girl has bones."

"Bummer, dude! Sorry to hear that. You got any plans to try to regain the throne?"

"Nope, I finally pulled off the Blindfolded Straight Jacket Parachute Escape. Nobody else has ever done it. Precious few have even survived it. I have a new throne now. I'm the best escape artist ever."

When Spineless left the show, he said that was his goal, but we all thought he just wanted to live in a country where he could smoke marijuana legally. I didn't know if I believed he'd really done it, but if he had, I was truly impressed. I saw nothing to be gained by doubting him about it.

"Congratulations! When's the coronation?"

"Sadly, the event is no longer sanctioned. Too many people died trying, but I don't care. The people who matter know I did it, even though YouTube banned the video."

"I'm happy for you, Dude," I told him honestly.

"Sam The Man says you got married, and left show business. I was hoping to hook up with you guys for a few shows while I was in town. Why would you marry somebody who wouldn't want to be married to The Absolutely Incredible Freak Show?"

"Actually, I quit show biz before I got married, not because I got married. But, I am planning one more performance. Can you meet me somewhere in the morning to talk about it?"

He answered quickly, "Sure. Will Starlight Lounge around ten work for you?"

Since Starlight is well known as one of the best bars in Dallas for day drinking, his suggestion didn't surprise me. Since it is also a short walk from my house, I readily agreed.

I'd spent the time recruiting focused entirely on the task at hand. Now, as I walked home, my imagination started going wild about what April might be going through. I tried to trust what Carl had told me about rules of combat, and how they wouldn't mistreat her unless they thought we weren't going to cooperate.

It didn't work, but it did get me thinking about all the things I might do to anybody who hurt her, and all the things I might let some of my friends and former co-stars do to them as well. They weren't exactly pleasant thoughts, but I found them comforting. I was still thinking them when I laid down hoping to sleep.

Surprisingly, I managed to get some sleep. When the alarm went off Tuesday morning at eight, it interrupted a dream that, even given the circumstances, only I would classify as a pleasant dream.

A few minutes after ten, I walked into The Starlight Lounge and saw Spicoli sitting at a table with a bottle of beer and an iPad in front of him. He was inhaling from a vaporizer. I seriously doubted that he was vaping a tobacco product, but I saw no reason to comment on it. Spicoli is famous, or at least infamous, for any number of tricks that he's performed.

If he had actually accomplished it, the Blindfolded Straight Jacket Parachute Escape probably tops that list. Even if he did, his ability to smoke weed and drink alcohol all day long and all night long without ever showing even the slightest sign of being affected by either is still impressive.

As I joined him at the table, he turned the tablet around to me, and a video started. In the video, two men on a helicopter put a blindfold and a straight jacket on Spicoli. The camera pans down to his ankles as one of the men straps a small bag to the ropes already binding his ankles. Spicoli dives out of the helicopter and free falls toward the earth.

He escapes the straight jacket, sheds it, takes the bag off his ankle, removes the parachute and straps it on his back. He pulls the cord and the chute opens. He floats down to earth safe and sound as he frees himself from the ankle binding.

I looked at him, "Is that the video YouTube pulled? I've seen much worse on there."

"That's the one. They said I could put it back if I made it clear that it was video trickery. Since it isn't video trickery, I couldn't do that."

"You could have been killed, Dude!"

"Could I? I know how to lose a straight jacket. I know how to put on a parachute. Any idiot can pull the cord on a parachute once it's on. The only way I die doing that trick is if I'm not who I claim to be, or if the chute malfunctions."

"Then why has nobody else been able to do it?"

"Because nobody else is Spineless Spicoli." He punctuated his statement by downing his beer and high-fiving me.

I had an idea about how to recruit Spicoli now. I wasn't sure if I could pull it off, but at least I had an idea. Spicoli has always been a bit of free spirit, a little flaky even by the standards of the freak show business.

"You have a plan on how to top that one?"

He looked surprised, "Top it? How do you top the greatest escape artist trick of all time?"

"I don't know. I have an idea, but it might really be dangerous. Are you up for some real danger going up against real threats?"

He laughed. "I live for danger, fear no man or beast...or however the Hell that goes. You'd think as many times as I've heard Bobbie Jo say that line, I'd have it memorized by now."

"Well it has been awhile. I'm talking real danger though, not the kind we are all so efficient at handling during a performance. What I'm working on at the moment isn't completely under our control."

"What do you mean by control?"

"I mean, that we don't get to set the scene. Somebody else set the scene, and may keep setting scenes. All we can control is how we react to it. The danger will be very real."

"Are you talking 'Most Dangerous Game' type stuff?"

"You could say that, but these guys aren't in it for sport. They're far more serious than that. It's not going to be enough to get away. We have to take them down."

Spicoli shook his head. "If anybody else was telling me this, I'd be laughing out loud, but you're serious; I can tell. How much are you getting paid for taking these guys on? More importantly, how much do you plan to pay me?"

I looked at him, until I was sure I had his attention, and his eyes met mine before I answered, "I'm not getting paid. I'm just trying to get my wife back alive. How much do you usually charge for helping rescue kidnapped women from international terrorists?"

Spicoli sat up straight, and shook out his arms the way he used to do before letting Rachel lock him into a straightjacket. "Dude, your wife's been kidnapped? Why didn't you say something earlier? Let's go rescue her. Where are they holding her?"

"It's not that simple. We don't know where she's being held, and we don't have a plan yet. Right now, I'm trying to put together an army, so when we find out where she is, we can rescue her."

He nodded.

I continued, "There's more to it than that. These guys are dangerous and deranged. Once we get her back, we still have to take them out to keep them from doing it again. Oh, and it's also possible that they may be planning to take out the US Government before they're done."

He shook his head. "You sure you aren't kidding?"

"I'm sure. I'm not exactly sure how we got into this mess, but we're in it. Do you want in it with us?"

"Hell, yes. Tell me all about it."

I gave him the Wikipedia version of our situation, by which I mean an extremely truncated and only partially accurate version. We didn't say anything else about money, but I knew if we all survived this, Spicoli would expect to be paid. Spineless always gets paid in one way or another.

19   Rational Phobia

I promised Spineless that he was in and that I'd be in touch and paid his tab. He made no move to get up, so I presumed he was going to cap off his morning with a few more beers. I'd let him pay for those himself. I started back to the office to let Carl know how the recruiting was going and see how he was doing.

I was almost back to the office when my phone rang. I saw it was Bobbie Jo as I answered, "Pegasus Investigations."

"I will never get used to professional entrepreneur Freak, but I must admit, you've got it down pat. I just talked to Jeff and I have something to show you. Can you come out here."

"I assume Jeff told you what's going on."

"He did. That's why I called. I'm going to help you get April back and perhaps a Hell of a lot more. Can you come out? My car's running again; I can come get you if you need a ride."

If I'd had any doubt that it was important, I didn't now. The only thing more unusual than Bobbie Jo having her old car in working order was her offering to drive it somewhere and risk it breaking down again.

I told her, "No need. I'll either find a ride or let DART do the walking for me."

"If your only ride is The Great Detective, take the blue line instead. I'll pick you up at the Downtown Garland Station."

It wasn't hard to guess what that meant. Bobbie Jo is perhaps the foremost spider enthusiast on the planet, and Carl is without a doubt the world's biggest arachnophobe. Whatever Bobbie Jo wanted to show me was going to have eight legs.

I called Sam the Man. He answered on the first ring. "That was quick. Where are the bad guys?"

"I don't know yet, just need a lift to one of the good guys this morning. The bastards kidnapped my chauffeur."

After a very quick courtesy laugh, Sam answered. "You know I'm going to have to charge you double now to not tell April you called her that as soon as we get her back, right?"

"No problem, can you take me out to Bobbie Jo's place this morning?"

"On my way, Kemosabe."

For a man who once said at my funeral that he barely spoke English, Osalumense has an extremely solid vocabulary of American slang. I was way too impressed to remember to tell him that my friends don't call me Kemosabe. Instead, I just told him to pick me up at my house, since it's closer to his place than the office.

It was about eleven thirty when Bobbie Jo let us into the house she still shares with her parents.

I couldn't remember the last time I'd been to her house. It was probably while we were still running The Absolutely Incredible Freak Show and Burlesque. I immediately noticed a new addition to the house. In one corner of what would have been the dining room if Bobbie Jo hadn't turned it into her hobby room, was a very large aquarium covered by a black cloth.

I pointed at it. "Damn, girl. If you've added enough spiders to your collection to justify a tank that big, I can see why you didn't want Carl to see it."

She pointed to some of her smaller tanks, including the one her prized tarantulas, Skipper and Skippette, call home. "You do realize that any one of these tanks would be reason not to invite him here, right?"

"Trudat! Why the cover on that one?"

"Two reasons; the main reason is because its inhabitant gives my mother the heebie jeebies. The second reason is that I'm a show girl. I want to make an impression on y'all when I introduce you to Miss Lickety Split."

Osalumense was grinning. "If Miss Lickety Split is big enough to justify a tank that size, I'm pretty sure she's going to make an impression on us."

Bobbie Jo laughed, "Oh big fella, you have no idea. Hasn't Rachel taught you that size isn't everything."

Like many conversations with Bobbie Jo, Osalumense, and any number of other friends, this one appeared to be sliding down hill fast. I normally don't mind. In fact, I'm often the reason for it, but I wasn't really in the mood.

"Your introduction was fabulous, are you going to introduce us or not?"

She smiled, "Oh yes!" She removed the cover, revealing that the tank was decorated like a turtle tank with lots of greenery and sand and stuff. I also noticed that unlike all her other tanks, this one was covered, and secured with two padlocks. The only thing I didn't immediately see was a spider.

A leaf moved, and then I saw her. Sam the Man saw her at the same time, and jumped back almost as quickly as Carl would have jumped. Miss Lickety Split was about twice as big as Skipper and Skippette. She also looked twice as fierce.

Even though I've grown accustomed to her pets over the years, I also jumped. That's because nothing else she'd ever shown me even began to compare to this beauty. It was like learning that your crazy cat loving friend had suddenly adopted a tiger.

Bobbie Jo was pleased with our reaction, "Any questions?"

I glanced at Osalumense, but he didn't seem ready to use words at that moment in time. I decided to ask the first two that came to mind. "What the Hell is that and do you really think you can train it?"

She had the glow she used to have on stage when she knew she was about to blow a crowd's mind, "Miss Lickety Split is a Brazilian Wandering Spider, also known as a Banana Spider. The term Banana Spider is not because she eats bananas, but because her natural habitat is the rain forests of Brazil, where her kind have killed thousands of banana pickers over the years."

Osalumense finally found a word, "Killed?"

"Yes, killed; the Brazilian Wandering Spider's venom is one of the most lethal toxins on earth. Her bite, because of her long fangs, is also one of the most painful. I presume you understand now why this tank is secured."

"Uh, yeah, but how does this help us get April back?"

She smiled, It was a smile that any man would appreciate, except perhaps Carl.

"It helps, my dear friend, because to answer your second question, I not only can train her. I have trained her."

"You told me years ago, that you don't train spiders, you adapt to them. Have you changed your mind?"

"Maybe, but more accurately, I've gotten better. Have a seat."

I noticed that Sam The Man found the barstool farthest away from Miss Lickety Split's tank. I sat in the stool beside him. If Bobbie Jo noticed, she was too polite to mention it.

"Training a spider is just like training a dog, or a lover for that matter?"

"Excuse me? I don't think you train lovers."

"Of course, you do. Let's say you want to train a lover to go with you on walks in the park and drink pina coladas. Yes, I know that song sucked, but work with me here. All you have to do is find a lover who likes walking in the park and drinking pina coladas."

"Uh, yeah, but…"

"But nothing, ever seen Charlie Ray's dog fetch a beer from the fridge? Of course, you have, it's my brother's favorite parlor trick. His dog is a Golden Retriever, they're bred to retrieve. All Charlie Ray had to do was put the beer in the right place, and teach the dog where it was."

"And how does this apply to spiders?"

"Well, you have to swear you'll never repeat this part, but it's really simple. All I had to do to train Skipper and Skippette to crawl on my body for an entire stage show was find two tarantulas that prefer to stay on the surface they're on rather than seeking out new ones. Since most tarantulas are like that, it was easy."

She smiled, "Have you never noticed in all the times you've sat for them, that when you put them on the table, they never leave the table unless you move them?"

"No, I guess I haven't, but how does this make you think you can train a Brazilian Wandering Spider not just to kill a human being, but to kill a particular human being?"

"I don't think I can. I already have. I know how this one hunts. I know what it seeks out. I guarantee you, I can make this one kill the one I want dead, if given the chance."

"And you're willing to bet your reputation on it?"

"I'm willing to bet my reputation and April's life. I know what I'm doing."

"Do I want to know what this one kills?"

"You're going to know whether you want to or not. She kills what I tell her to kill, when I tell her to kill it."

92

I looked at her face, hoping to see some hint of amusement or whimsy. What I saw was the same conviction Ezekiel has when he preaches. That comforted me just a little, until I remembered that it was also the same certainty that Charlie Manson and the Son of Sam have been known to display.

20   Pavlovian Pets

"Please, Gentlemen settle in as The Queen of Danger presents her Magnum Opus in the underappreciated field of Arachnoid Conditioning. Any in the audience with weak hearts or squeamish minds would be well advised to skip today's presentation in favor of a more genteel entertainment."

Osalumense and I clapped to be polite. As we did so, Bobbie Jo retrieved a mason jar from underneath one of the other tanks and removed a small gecko. With the gecko in one hand she unlatched a small slot in the top of Miss Lickety Split's cage. She dropped the gecko into the tank, and wasted no time securing the tank.

Bobbie Jo continued, "The gecko is just as common in the Brazilian rainforest as it is in the United States, but without the unfortunate tendency to show up in television commercials for cut-rate insurance companies. It is also considered quite a delicacy for the Brazilian Wandering Spider."

The gecko seemed somewhat interested in not getting anywhere near Bobbie Jo's spider. Miss Lickety Split, on the other hand, seemed completely disinterested in its presence. I presumed the spider had either not noticed it, or simply wasn't hungry. While my eyes were on the tank, Bobbie Jo returned the jar to its place and picked up something that looked like an executive type pen.

"You'll note that Miss Lickety Split has been presented a delicacy, but chooses not to enjoy. This is the mark of a well trained pet. Much like a Labrador Retriever must learn to act against his instinct to be a good hunting dog, my little friend has been trained to obey her instinct only when I tell her to do so."

With that, she walked back to the other tank and pulled a live cricket from another mason jar. I know almost as little about hunting dogs as I know about Banana Spiders, and I strongly suspected that my friend, Sam The Man, knew even less than I did. We nodded, smiled and waited for her to get back.

Like she had with the gecko, she opened the top of the tank and dropped the cricket into it. Again, she wasted no time securing the tank, "The cricket is also common in Brazil, where many natives believe they have the power to foretell the future. I don't deal much in omens, but I can certainly predict the future of this one cricket with one hundred percent accuracy."

I laughed, "I don't think you have to be a soothsayer to tell that things don't look good for the cricket or the gecko."

"Perhaps, even a fraud like Miss Cleo could predict that Miss Lickety Split would be dining soon, but I'm not a fraud. Even Siegfried and Roy couldn't always accurately predict their tigers' next meal. I can, and I can assure that for today, anyway, that gecko is the safest thing in this room."

"I'm not sure the gecko would agree with that assessment."

"Nonetheless, I stand by it. Are you ready for me to demonstrate?"

Sam The Man continued to lean back on his barstool as far back as a seven foot tall, three hundred pound man can lean away from that tank without turning and running for his life. He managed to speak, "Sure, my dear, I can't wait."

She held the pen slightly above the tank and clicked it. The pen turned out to be a laser pointer with a green light. Although the glass of the tank diffused it a little she was able to point it toward the bottom of the tank near Miss Lickety Split. The spider reacted almost immediately. Her body lifted slightly and her back four legs tensed up.

Sam The Man also tensed a bit. He didn't run away, but that was probably because he didn't want me to be able to mock him for it. He didn't realize that I would never mock him for it, since I probably would have been right behind him.

Bobbie Jo smiled, "I see you noticed that Miss Lickety Split is ready for my command. The second act won't last long, don't blink."

We nodded. She slid the green dot across the tank until it lightly touched the cricket's left hind leg. I didn't blink, but I really wish I had. The spider crossed the tank in a heartbeat and the cricket didn't survive much longer. If I had blinked, I wouldn't even be able to testify that the meal Miss Lickety Split was savoring had once been a cricket.

Bobbie Jo turned her pen light off and beamed, "You did note that she chose the meal I pointed out to her over her preferred diet, didn't you? The cricket died due to the incisions of her fangs not her poison, but her poison kills almost as quickly and her fangs are so long and so sharp that most humans go into shock from the pain while the poison finishes them off. As for the gecko, it will sleep safely, if nervously, in the tank unless I point her out for Miss Lickety Split, or fail to provide another alternate for too many days."

She retrieved the cover, and put it back over the tank. Osalumense relaxed considerably and said, "You didn't need to cover it. Freak and I aren't squeamish."

"Of course, you aren't. Like most great hunters, Miss Lickety Split prefers to nap after a meal."

"Of course," I said. "I can't deny that I'm impressed, a little worried about you, but definitely impressed. How exactly does this help us get April back and defeat the enemy army?"

"I thought I'd just demonstrated that. Don't tell me we plan to win all the battles it's going to take to win the war without killing any of the enemy. This is real life, not a lame television series."

"No, we'll kill as many people as it takes, but I was thinking the arsenal of assault rifles we're putting together might be more efficient than trying to have a spider bite everybody we don't like."

For about two seconds, she looked crestfallen. Then, she broke into the smile she always used on stage right as one of our acts was about to change from the unbelievable to the impossible.

"You don't mind if I keep Miss Lickety Split in training in case you change your mind, do you?"

"Of course not, if nothing else we can use her to help interrogate any prisoners we end up taking. The Great Detective may be the world's most arachnophobic person, but he's a member of a very large fraternity of them. A fraternity, I might add, that will probably increase considerably if you get many opportunities to show her off."

"Thank you, kind sir. But I think you may be forgetting something about guns. My brother and I have been shooting guns since we were children, I know a little bit about them."

"I'll bite, what am I forgetting?"

Her smile had become a Cheshire cat grin, "Guns don't kill people; they only make bullets go really, really fast. And a bullet that hits an arm or a leg or an ironically positioned dog tag doesn't kill anybody, either. If my girl gets a chance at even a pinky toe, then that toe is attached to a dead person. You don't have a gun in your arsenal that can do that, do you?"

I didn't bother telling her that I didn't exactly have the arsenal, yet. I did, however, make a mental note that Charlie Ray and Bobbie Jo were both experienced with guns. The fact that they grew up in the real city that became Hank Hill's hometown in the television series 'King of the Hill' meant that I probably should have assumed that.

"Okay, I'll include Miss Lickety Split as part of our arsenal when the actual battles begin."

She crossed her arms acting like she was upset just the way she used to do it as part of our show whenever she pretended that nobody was whipping me hard enough. The only difference was that she was smiling this time, "She should be listed as on-call personnel. Her fangs can be listed as arsenal and her venom as a consumable with no replacement cost."

I laughed, "Done. I do have one condition, though."

"What's the condition?"

"We absolutely, positively do not ever let The Great Detective know about any of this!"

She laughed, "Agreed."

Just like that, one of the most deadly, and even I'll admit most frightening creatures on the face of the earth had been imported from South America to join our increasingly diverse and formidable army in the fight against international terrorists.

It surprised me tremendously, but I was actually beginning to like our chances. As soon as Mistress Caroline provided us with a more traditional arsenal, I would be ready for battle. I knew some of the soldiers could use some more training, and I was glad she was going to provide it. But, I also felt I had enough trained soldiers to mount the first attack.

The first attack, of course was the rescue of April. With sharpshooters, detectives, cops, bouncers, dominatrices, gunnery sergeants, arachnologists and one superhero on our team, I felt we were ready.

I know my curse isn't actually a superpower, but I've relied on it for many years in a multitude of tough spots, and it hasn't let me down so far. If I had known at that moment that my superpowers would be of no value, and April's rescue was going to succeed or fail based on the effectiveness of the soldier I trusted least, my confidence would have more accurately reflected our reality.

21 Brute Force

Thursday morning at ten, I was at home desperately wishing I knew where the bad guys were, so my new army could go to battle. I knew we weren't much of an army, didn't have an arsenal and hadn't even begun training; but I was getting anxious. I was so antsy that I actually jumped when my home phone rang.

I could pretend I jumped because nobody calls that phone to talk to me, and nobody calls April except when she's here to answer it, but the reality is that I was on edge. It took four rings for me to find the handset, but I found it in the kitchen by the stove. I answered professionally, "Pegasus Investigations."

Rachel laughed, "This is your home phone, Freak. You don't have to answer it like that."

"I guess not, but it's kind of become a habit. What's up?"

"She has something she wants to show you. Can I come get you?"

When Rachel uses pronouns as identifiers, they might as well be proper names. 'He' is always her husband, my good friend Osalumense. 'She' is always her boss, Mistress Caroline. I don't think Mistress Caroline is my good friend, but she's definitely good at what she does.

"Of course," I answered.

"Good, I'm almost downtown now. I'll pick you up in a couple of minutes."

True to her word, she was in front of my house a few minutes later. As I closed the passenger door and reached for the seatbelt, I asked, "Are you at liberty to tell me what it is she wants to show me?"

Again, she laughed. Nothing about her laugh has changed in the years that have passed since she and I quit dating and both married other people.

"I am, and I will. She says you asked for guns. She got you guns."

I tried not to sound too excited, "Cool."

"Oh, how I used to love cavalier, nothing impresses me much, Freak Show. How much you want to bet you can't keep up the façade and not act impressed once you see it?"

"I'll pass. Do you want to give me a hint, or do I have to wait until we get there?"

She laughed again, "I just gave you the hint. Feel free to let your imagination run wild while I drive."

I don't actually need permission to let my imagination run wild, but it usually doesn't. If Mistress Caroline had acquired anything for our arsenal more impressive than Bobby Jo's Miss Lickety Split, I would feel free to be totally impressed. After all, I didn't take Rachel's bet. She drove to the dungeon where she and her boss ply their craft in the comfortable silence that longtime friends often share, and lovers almost never do.

As everybody in the BDSM community and almost nobody outside of it knows, dungeons tend to relocate somewhat regularly. Mistress Caroline's dungeon is currently located just off the Dallas North Tollway very close to the Dallas County – Denton County border.

The Great Detective and I enjoy the irony of the fact that this puts it a stone's throw from the largest Baptist church in North Texas. I've never asked Rachel or Mistress Caroline if they agreed, and I never will. It was almost eleven when Rachel led me past an empty receptionist desk and back to the huge room the staff referred to as the play room.

As I walked in, I realized I should have taken Rachel's bet. The word 'impressed' so completely didn't cover my reaction to what I saw that she would have had no choice to admit that I'd won the bet. Amazingly, the arsenal isn't what first blew me away. In the northeast corner of the room where a suspension rack normally hung, there were now three racks with human target dummies suspended.

They looked a little like the crash test dummies from the television ads, but they had targets drawn on both their heads and torsos. I also noticed a pile of replacements behind them. Obviously, Mistress Caroline was taking her role as Gunnery Sergeant and her dungeon's role as training ground seriously.

I was still staring at the dummies when Mistress Caroline put her hand gently on my shoulder and led me toward the side room that serves as a changing room for her girls, as well as a storage room for their toys. "You're missing the best part."

I long ago concluded that Mistress Caroline didn't know how to do anything gently, but apparently I was wrong. As my eyes took in the room, my mind began to search for words: astounded, shocked, dumbfounded and stunned all came to mind. Each of these words seemed grossly inadequate.

I didn't take a complete inventory, but as I looked around I saw five different rocket launchers, including one that looked just like the bazooka I had gotten to use once at an ROTC camp in high school. I also saw at least ten sniper rifles, similar to the one that shot me in downtown Dallas a few years ago, and three crossbows.

I didn't even try to count the AK-47's, Uzi's, semi automatic pistols, M14s or K-Gar knifes, but I saw enough to know that my army was barely large enough to carry all of them somewhere, let alone wield them all. I also saw more than a handful of weapons I couldn't even identify.

I turned to look at Mistress Caroline, "Which country do we plan to overtake after I get April back, and will we make enough money off it to help me pay for all this?"

Mistress Caroline smiled. It was the same smile she always smiled; the one that helped convince me that gentle wasn't in her repertoire, "Relax, my dear boy, we didn't buy everything you see. We only have to pay for the ammo we use, and anything we can't return after we get April back."

"Where the Hell did you get all this?"

She put her forefinger to my lips, again gently, "Shush. Don't ask questions that don't help you get what you want. I got them, therefore, we have them. That is all that matters at the moment; that, and perhaps, the fact that I can get more if we need them."

"Great, but we won't need more. My army isn't near large enough to use half of what you already have, let alone need more."

"Your army may not be, but if it comes to it, our army will be. I told you earlier that you could never completely understand what I'm talking about. I didn't mean it as an insult then, and I still don't. April will be rescued or she will be avenged. I allow you to command our army in part because it is your fight as much as mine, in part because Rachel trusts you and in part because I find you to be both tolerant and tolerable."

I wasn't sure completely what she meant, but I was completely sure that she meant it completely.

She continued, "But, make no mistake, Freak, my army is fully committed. We will not lose this war. Either April comes home alive to her loving husband, or there will be Hell to pay. That arsenal is nothing compared to what my army can and will bring. Do you understand and agree?"

"I understand. But there is no 'or.' April is coming home. That is my only objective."

Mistress Caroline held out her hand and I shook it.

"Agreed," she said. "You can send your people for training at any time. This training facility will be open 24/7 until April is home."

"Thank you," I said.

"Rachel, please take him home, or wherever he needs to go. You have a client at two-thirty. Don't dawdle."

As we got in her car, I asked Rachel to take me to the house. When we were on the road, I asked, "Do you have any idea where she got all that?"

"If I did, I wouldn't be at liberty to reveal it. I probably wouldn't even be at liberty to reveal that I know it."

I laughed, "Of course not."

22   Amazing Ray

Rachel dropped me off about one-thirty. I went to the fridge to see what I could turn into lunch. The phone rang before I'd made a decision. I glanced at the caller ID before I answered. "Hey, Boss, What's up?"

"I'm still not your boss. Have you talked to Amazing, yet?"

Amazing, of course, is my friend Ray, who performed in the Absolutely Incredible Freak Show Revue and Burlesque under the name of The Amazing Raymond. He also holds the honor of being the only former costar that I never once considered recruiting for this battle.

"Uh, no, I haven't yet. Do we need him?"

"I do, I'm going out of town for a few days, and I want him to come with me."

"You're going out of town, now?! Where are you going?"

"I'm taking Emily and Jade to a safe house. I'd tell you where it is, but then I'd have to... well, you understand."

"Of course, and you need Raymond for that to make sure you can find the safe house later. Do you have any thoughts on how to convince him to sign up?"

"I always have thoughts, Freak. You know that. My thought is that I call you and tell you I need him, and then you convince him to do it."

I laughed, and hung up without bothering to tell him that nobody calls me Freak or that he knows more about training spiders than I know about how to convince Raymond to do things. All I could do was ask Raymond what might currently motivate him to leave the house and hope I had a way to provide it.

In recent years, The Amazing Raymond has reacted to my phone calls when he doesn't want to talk to me by either refusing to answer the phone or answering just to make sure he had the chance to cuss at me and hang up on me. With that in mind, I decided to call from a phone that he wouldn't know was me.

Interestingly, at other times in recent years, he's been happy to hear from me, but I thought it wiser not to assume that would be the case. Unfortunately, the days when there was a payphone on every corner are long since past, relegated to the movies that were made when you actually needed a story line and some people who could act to get a film made.

Fortunately, I knew a place nearby where I could use a phone that wouldn't identify me. I walked the few blocks from my house to the Center for Community Cooperation thinking of what I might be able to use to entice Raymond to accompany Carl on his trip, but I couldn't think of anything.

As I walked onto the property, a few dozen memories of my first trip to this place came flooding back. At the time, the visit had been a really bad day, but although it's not true that time heals all wounds, it certainly helps. I walked into the lobby, and saw Lisha sitting at the desk where she's been sitting for many years.

Her husband, Rick Woodbury, is now earning far too much money from the Dallas Police Department, largely thanks to The Great Detective and me, for her to need to keep working, but she likes her job, so she hasn't quit. She looked up from her computer screen as I crossed the lobby and smiled. It was a smile that hurt like hell the first time I saw it, but today I just returned it.

"Can I borrow a phone?"

"Of course, Freak." She pointed at the phone on her desk. "Will this one work, or do you need privacy?"

"Privacy might be better, plus I'm not sure how long the call might last."

She nodded toward an office behind her and returned to her computer screen. I followed her lead into the office and closed the door behind me. I sat in the executive chair behind the executive desk in the big executive office of the Center for Community Cooperation and reached for the phone.

As I dialed, I wondered briefly what an executive does here to justify such fine furniture. The Amazing Raymond answered fairly quickly in the slightly bored tone he almost always uses when he decides to actually answer his phone. "Hello."

"It's Freak. Please don't hang up!" I said as quickly as I could in the hopes of finishing before he hung up on me. The effort was apparently wasted.

"Hang up? Surely, you jest. I have been nervously waiting for this call, as you once put it so eloquently, like an unattractive teenage girl awaits a call as prom night approaches."

I had no recollection of ever saying anything like that, but I'm far too intelligent to question The Amazing Raymond's memory on anything. Besides, it had to bode well for my chance of convincing him to accompany Carl that he'd been waiting for my call.

"Should I ask why you've been anxiously awaiting my call?"

"If you don't know, I suppose you should. I would have thought you'd already know. You are putting the band back together, right?"

"I'm not sure that's exactly the way I'd have put it, but I guess so. We're not doing a show, though. This is much more serious than that."

"I know that, Freak. I know April has been kidnapped, I know you are putting the band back together to go get her, and I plan to help in any way possible. I gave up show business long before you did, but neither of us gave up being absolutely incredible or amazing."

I was far too happy to learn that he was eager to help to wonder how he knew what was going on. We call him the Amazing Raymond mostly because he remembers every single thing that he sees, hears or reads. That part of his mind may not even be its most amazing feature, though.

"Well, the first thing we want you to do isn't very glamorous, but it may be important. Carl is going on a trip, and he'd like you to join him."

He laughed, "Well, that doesn't sound glamorous or important, but we both know Carl well enough to know that if he says it's important, it is very likely to be important."

I didn't bother to tell him that it was me that said it was important, not Carl. Instead I just told him to expect a call from Carl and thanked him for helping us. Carl wouldn't have asked me to get Ray to go with him if he didn't think it might be important, so I wasn't really lying about it. The fact that I didn't think it would be important didn't matter. It also may explain why nobody calls me The Great Detective.

Part 5 – Captive Beauty

"LORD, I cry unto thee: make haste unto me;
Give ear unto my voice, when I cry unto thee.
Let my prayer be set forth before thee as incense;
And the lifting up of my hands as the evening sacrifice…

Keep me from the snares which they have laid for me
And the gins of the workers of iniquity.."

Psalm 141
David

23 Road Trip

I don't know how long I'd been in captivity before I woke up, or where we were when I woke up. I also didn't know where we were three hours later when the van came to a stop for the first time. I was pretty sure it was three hours away and somewhat west of wherever I was when I woke up

That information wasn't likely to help, but it was all I'd learned. The Russians spoke Russian and ignored me. I suspected if I'd tried to start a conversation, they'd have let me, but I saw nothing to be gained from that.

The man driving got out of the van and closed his door gently. Seconds later he opened the back door of the van and climbed in the cargo hold with me. I noticed that he didn't hurry at all. He clearly wasn't worried about anybody seeing him or me and suspecting foul play. That meant screaming wouldn't help and would only serve to make them mad.

He closed the door behind him.

"No scream for help, Dear? You are a very interesting young lady. Don't you want to escape?"

I smiled what I hoped what was an enigmatic smile, "Escape? If I do that I might miss seeing the exciting conclusion. No, thanks, I want my front row seat for that."

"As I said, you are a very interesting young lady, but just in case you're lying, I'm afraid I'm going to have to make sure you don't yell at the wrong moment."

His method of assuring my silence was to stuff a ridiculously large ball gag in my mouth, and then cover it and my entire head with a leather hood. He was careful, even gentle as he did it. He made sure I wouldn't choke and my breathing through the nose hole was normal before he left.

I'm sure some of Rachel's clients would really enjoy this particular situation. I didn't, but I could handle it, if I had to, and I obviously had to handle it for the moment. It would have been nice if the hood had eye holes in addition to the nose hole, but a girl can't have everything.

Brian D. Eyre

The van started moving again. A few minutes and several turns later, it stopped. With the hood on, I couldn't tell who was where or what doors were being opened or closed. A few minutes later, I felt hands on my head. The hood and the gag were removed.

They were removed much less gently than they'd been put on, but at least they were removed. I saw immediately that the man who had been driving was in the cargo hold with me and the other man was driving. I wondered if they were setting the stage for good cop, bad cop, but I said nothing.

"You're allowed to talk, Doll Face."

I didn't say anything. The Great Detective would be proud of me if I lived long enough to tell him about my performance. My kidnapper grew tired of the silence quickly.

"In fact, I encourage you to talk. When we don't want you to talk, you will be gagged so that you can not talk."

I noted that he was encouraging me to talk. If someone wants you to talk, it usually means they want to learn something from you. If someone kidnaps you in broad daylight and ties you up in the back of a van for a long ride, it's safe to assume that what they want to learn is important enough to try not to let them learn it.

This is not a part I ever wanted to play, but at least I had a grasp on what role I needed to play.

"Don't call me, Doll Face." I said it with as much force as such an inane comment can be said. The best way to beat a lie detector if you don't happen to be a sociopath is to confuse the baseline. It wasn't a great script, but it was one I felt confident I could play out, even if things got rough.

"I don't think you're in a position to tell me what to call you, Doll Face."

"Sure I am."

He said something to the other man in Russian, but got no answer.

"How are you in position to tell me what to call you?"

"You said you were encouraging me to speak, so I spoke. I don't like being called Doll Face, so I told you not to call me Doll Face."

110

"That's good to know, Doll Face. I can tell we're going to get along just fine."

I doubted that very much, but I saw no reason to mention it. I hoped it was a good sign that he truly believed I didn't like being called Doll Face. If I was going to need to tell some big lies later, it was good to know that he'd believed my first little lie.

I was now in character and ready to play my role. Now, if I could just find a way to survive the final scene.

24   Familiar Face

"I'm going to need you to wake up now, Sleepy Head. We have to get going."

This voice had no accent, or at least, no Russian accent. He was certainly American, and almost as certainly, not Southern. I turned toward the source of the voice and saw the face I expected to see the first time I woke up in the back of this van.

I hadn't actually been asleep, but I didn't mention that. I concentrated on not showing any hint that I'd recognized him.

"You don't remember me. I'm hurt."

I smiled, "I'm sorry. I've been under a wee bit of stress lately. Where should I know you from?"

I heard both Russians laughing from the van's front seat, but kept my gaze on the American in the back with me.

He smiled and reached into the fanny pack he was wearing.

"Perhaps this will remind you."

He pulled out a gun, which I immediately realized was mine. Of course, since I knew who he was, I knew how he got it.

'Hey!" I said in my shocked tone of voice. "That's my gun. How did you get it?"

He grinned. "We took it when we kidnapped you, Doll Face. Don't you remember that part?"

I didn't answer, and he didn't insist on it. Instead, he continued. "It doesn't matter. All that matters is that we have it and we have you. Do you understand your situation?"

"I understand that you have me. I don't understand why."

"I know that. I'm going to explain it to you. My associates' English is far short of fluent, and we feared there might be a communication problem if they tried to explain it you. It isn't exactly complicated, but it's extremely important that you understand it correctly."

I nodded.

He said something in Russian to his associates, and they both got out. I didn't know if that was a good sign or a bad sign, so I just accepted it without comment.

"Alone at last," he said. My name is Cliff Parsons, you may call me Cliff. May I call you April?"

"Sure, Cliff. I'd shake your hand, but I'm a little tied up at the moment."

"Indeed, you are. It is an unfortunate, but unavoidable consequence of the current circumstance. Let me explain it to you. Your boss, Mr. Jennings, has something that belongs to my associates and I. We want it back, and he seems reluctant to return it. Are you following me so far?"

"I'm following you just fine, but if you are looking for somebody to believe that Carl Jennings stole something of yours, you kidnapped the wrong girl."

He laughed. "Don't worry about that, we've got the right girl. You're right about Mr. Jennings. I'm sorry if I implied that he had stolen it. We both know he is not capable of such an act. It was stolen by an extremely dishonest man and given to Mr. Jennings for safe keeping. He has kept it safe, but he refuses to return it to its rightful owners."

"Did you ask him nicely before you kidnapped his receptionist?"

"We both know you are more than just a receptionist, but to answer your question, yes. We asked him very nicely. You know he can be quite stubborn, don't you?"

"I do know that. Do you really think that kidnapping me will make him less stubborn?"

"I don't know; it might or it might not. I hope for your sake that it either makes him less stubborn or makes it not matter."

I waited for him to explain what that meant, but he either wasn't interested in explaining or he was waiting for me to ask. If it was the latter, I disappointed him. My plan was to keep disappointing him until Freak came charging in to rescue me.

"So, April, the most important question right now is 'are you going to cooperate with me or fight me?' I promise you, it will be in your best interest to cooperate."

"I believe you." I told him honestly. Then I lied, "I'll cooperate."

113

"Good, I'm going to need you to let me do something. I need to put contacts in your eyes. They will make it impossible for you to see until I take them out, but if you behave while you have them in, I'll take them out for you."

"You want to do that so you can take me some place where there might be witnesses, right?"

"Yes, the other option is to knock you out again and carry you. We can do that if you prefer."

"No, that would be inconvenient for you, and I said I would cooperate. You can put the contacts in."

He put them in gently, like a well trained and caring ophthalmologist. As he promised, I could not see a thing once they were in. I hoped he'd also keep his promise to take them out.

He released my bondage and helped me out of the van, holding onto my arm tightly in a manner that I'm sure looked from a distance to be caring and loving.

He whispered in my ear, "In case you decide to make a break for it, I should warn you. We are walking a few feet from a giant hole in the ground. If you run in the wrong direction you will fall unceremoniously to your death."

I didn't ask what would happen if I ran in the right direction, but he answered it anyway.

"And if you guess right and miss the hole you will die by sniper fire at the hands of one or more of my associates."

Part 6 – Homeland Insecurity

"She's the sweetest rose of color this soldier ever knew,
Her eyes are bright as diamonds; they sparkle like the dew;
You may talk about your Dearest May, and sing of Rosa Lee,
But the Yellow Rose of Texas beats the belles of Tennessee.

Oh now I'm going to find her, for my heart is full of woe,
And we'll sing the songs together that we sung so long ago."

Yellow Rose of Texas
J.K.

25   Guard Detail

"How long are we supposed to guard the fortress while Freak and his Scooby Gang play army and you drive around the country?" Jeff didn't sound concerned, which didn't surprise me since he never sounds concerned.

"At least three or four days, I'm not really sure. Freak and his guys will be close by if you need them, but you won't need them. As you know, the fortress pretty much guards itself."

Jeff smiled at me from behind the desk in the lobby. He held up the remote that controlled the office's features. "And if they kill me and take this, then what?"

"Then you don't have to guard the fortress any longer, and some bad guys are going to be really pissed off. That remote doesn't access the secret stair case, and the one that does is in a place they will never find and couldn't take if they did find it. Don't make them kill you over this one, okay?"

"I'll try to stay alive until you get back. Do I get hazard pay on this one?"

I laughed, "I'm pretty sure we all get hazard pay on this one. It kind of makes me wish hazard pay was more than our regular rate, but it isn't. This isn't like the real army."

He favored me with a courtesy laugh. "Neither is the real Army. Get out of here, Boss. I've got this. You need to get the girls to safety and interrogate the Hell out of the Federal Government. I wish I had your assignment instead of mine, but you're the boss."

I certainly understood how a young, single man might think driving across the country with three beautiful ladies and a human tape recorder might be a more choice assignment than pretending to guard an office that couldn't possibly be in less need of guarding. I didn't share his enthusiasm, but I won't deny that I was looking forward to it a little.

Amazing Raymond had gone to pick up the rental car while I gave Jeff his redundant marching orders, or more accurately non-marching orders. Jeff and anybody he decided to hire to help him were going to pretend to guard the office until the situation was resolved, so Freak and I would be free to devote our time elsewhere.

I don't how many operatives with Jeff's talents would have accepted such a menial assignment without complaint. I do know that Freak and I were damn happy to have him onboard for this. At 9:14, Raymond called to tell me he had the rental and was parked in front of the office.

I grabbed the two suitcases I had already packed and went to the door. As I opened it, Jeff said, "Tell Raymond I'm expecting a word for word account of every insult you hit the Feds with."

"I'll tell him, but he'll remember every single one even if I don't." I didn't bother telling Jeff that I wasn't planning to hit the Feds with any insults. I figured it was better to leave Jeff with something enjoyable to anticipate.

Amazing was still sitting in the driver's seat of the Cadillac Escalade SUV when I started down the stairs. He opened the rear hatch as I got downstairs, and I put my two suitcases in beside his backpack. I was not surprised to see that he was traveling light. Show business types are famous for being able to travel light. I got in the Caddy on the passenger side, and he started her up.

"Are we still picking up the ladies at the Jack Evans Police Building?"

"Yes. Emily parked in the east lot. Drop me off in front and go find her SUV. I'll go get them and bring them down. Courtney is sure her people have security under control for this part of the trip."

"Do you trust her?"

"I trust her as much as I've ever trusted any government employee."

He laughed, "In other words, 'no.' What's our next destination after that?"

I told him the name of our first destination.

"Great! They really have a safe house in a city with only 31,830 people?"

Without letting on that I might be impressed, I said, "Apparently."

"Do we have a decent cover story that will explain why I have to be with you for the entire trip and for every meeting? Are we still planning to go with me as your personal bodyguard?"

"I am, unless you have a better plan."

118

He shook his head. "I don't even have a plan that isn't as good, which is pretty incredible considering how bad that plan is."

"It's not as bad a plan as you think it is. Courtney knows I met you through Freak. You may think of Freak as an ordinary guy who happens not to feel pain and used to make a living being tortured."

I gave him some time to admit that he knew that Freak wasn't exactly ordinary, but as I expected he declined to comment one way or the other on the subject.

I continued, "Trust me on this, the Dallas Police Department, the Department of Homeland Security and Courtney's agency don't view him that way. If Freak or I introduced them to a stray kitten that Emily found in our alley and told them it was a terrorist operative, at least two Federal Agencies would follow that poor kitten for the rest of its life."

"Okay, I get it. I suppose I even slightly believe it. I only have one problem. I spent all night trying to think of a good alias for this, and I don't have one. Apparently, whatever chemical imbalance causes my brain to remember every detail prevents it from making up any details."

I'd never considered that. I thought about asking him if he'd never lied, but decided this wasn't the time for that. Instead, I decided I better come up with an alias for him. Since we were already on South Lamar just north of the Jack Evans Police Building, I needed to do it quickly.

He parked where I had told him to park, and I got out of the Caddy. "Rick Blaine," I told him as I started to close the door.

As I walked toward the front entrance, I heard him yell, "Richard, Damn it! Nobody's called me Rick since I closed the Cabaret."

The Amazing Raymond's disinterest in classic movies is as total as my love for them, but apparently, at least once in his life he read or heard something that mentioned that Humphrey Bogart's character in Casablanca had been named Rick Blaine and had owned a cabaret.

I made a mental note to ask him if he'd ever actually seen the movie, but I didn't expect to ever do it. Asking him simple questions like that often ends up taking far more time than it should. I once asked him if he knew anything about the musical Les Miserable's, and he spent almost forty-five minutes on the subject.

Fortunately, I'd been wise enough to duck out of the conversation a few minutes into his dissertation. Unfortunately, I learned later that his entire body of knowledge on the subject was skewed by the fact that he'd never actually seen the musical or the movie.

I put that thought out of my mind as I climbed the stairs to Lieutenant Underwood's office to collect the girls. Raymond's social skills have improved dramatically in recent years. He's still not exactly Beau Geste, but he at least understands social conventions, and generally follows them whenever possible.

That's why I optimistically expected our road trip to take place without an Amazing Ray filibuster. I turned out to be wrong about that, but a filibuster isn't always a bad thing.

26   Olive Branch

With everything packed, we got in the SUV. Courtney insisted on riding shotgun, and Raymond insisted on driving. The ladies and I sat in the back seat. The miles passed without incident for several hours. What conversation occurred was light, casual and involved blessedly little input from Raymond or me.

Jade and Emily carried on several conversations with topics ranging from sights they hoped to see on this trip to card games or other amusements they could find while they were sequestered for their own safety. If I didn't know better, I might have thought the ladies were not taking the danger that they faced seriously, but I knew better.

If Courtney had any concern, she gave no sign. An agent assigned to protect a civilian or multiple civilians has to walk a fine line between understating the danger and inducing total panic. I had made it clear, and Courtney had readily agreed that my people were in charge of protecting the civilians. Her job was to provide a safe house, support and intelligence.

At 2:34, Raymond pulled us over into the Arkansas side of Texarkana so we could change rentals. That accomplished, we got something to eat, and then changed rentals again. It's not paranoia if they really are out to get you. As we'd agreed, I took over the driving at that point.

Raymond sat behind me. The others kept their original seats. Once we were back on the road, the conversation turned in a direction that made me uncomfortable. It started slowly during a pause in Jade and Emily's discussion of strategies for winning at forty-two.

At first, it seemed Courtney just wanted to involve Raymond and be sociable. By the time we got to Little Rock, I knew with reasonable certainty that Courtney doubted Raymond's cover story, and was vetting his credentials. I guessed she'd just been biding her time until he wasn't driving.

In other circumstances, it might have been fun to hear Raymond dodging questions. After all the man has made some pretty good money, not to mention a reputation both good and bad, for his ability and eagerness to answer any question. Today, I wasn't expecting to have any fun at all.

As we neared Forest City, I spoke. "I don't really care how Mr. Blaine got into the security industry. I'm just happy that, thanks to Freak, we have him on the Pegasus Investigations team. If the man doesn't want to talk about how he ended up in his present career, I would really expect everybody in this car to understand and respect that he chooses not to talk about it. After all, we're all in the not talking too much business in one way or another."

Courtney laughed, "Touche! Was I prying? I'm sorry! I suppose it's an occupational hazard. I can't deny that I'm curious about your career path and skill set. I don't mean to pry. It's just that I see very few people in my size range working that phase of the business, no offense intended."

In the time I'd known Raymond, I'd never seen him get upset about his size or any comment made about his size. However, I also couldn't think of many times anybody had ever insulted him about it, either. I hoped this wouldn't be one of them.

It wasn't, "No offense taken, ma'am. In fact, I'm honored that you noticed. You see, my size is one reason I drifted into this field. What kind of man would I be if I chose a career simply because my body type seems to fit it? Who would want to go through life living the life somebody decided they should live because of their physical characteristics?"

I didn't think Raymond knew any details about Courtney's past, but I couldn't deny that he'd hit a nerve. She nodded as she looked accusingly at me, but I was driving and didn't acknowledge her. Besides, Raymond was just getting warmed up, and when he's on, he's a joy to behold.

"Consider, if you will, the career of Anthony Jerome Webb of Dallas, Texas. Born in the summer of 1963, a few short months before the tragic death of John Fitzgerald Kennedy, young Anthony seemed to all who met him to be a fine young man with an unrealistic dream. You see, while attending Wilmer-Hutchins High School, Anthony foolishly told anybody who would listen that he planned to play in the National Basketball Association."

Emily was again right on cue. "Why was that foolish? Was he not a good basketball player?"

"Good question, Emily. Anthony was a good enough basketball player, but he stood only five foot, seven inches tall, if that. High school teams traditionally add a few inches to the listed heights of smaller athletes, for some unknown reason. But even if Anthony, or Spud, as he came to be known was every inch of his listed height, he was far too short to play in the NBA."

"Did he ever make it?" I'm not sure if Jade was playing the role or really didn't know. Her husband had played college basketball, but that was a long time ago, and I've never heard Jade discuss the sport at all, so I don't know if she's ever followed it. Either way, it was the perfect prompt.

"Oh, did he ever? Spud not only made it to The Association, he lasted long enough to play 814 games, score 8,072 points and perhaps most surprisingly, block 111 opposing shots. Oh, and by the way, he also won the Slam Dunk Contest at the 1986 All-Star Game."

Courtney clapped. "I get it now. You didn't have the range shooting basketballs to make it as a professional basketball player, so you chose bodyguard as a profession so you could shoot guns instead of jumpers."

Raymond smiled courteously, and told some stories of other undersized professionals. Doug Flutie, and Danica Patrick, I had heard of before. Several of the boxers, wrestlers and soldiers, I didn't know at all. He told all the stories to a rapt audience. If anybody thought he'd made any of it up, nobody suggested it.

By the time we left Memphis southbound on I-240, I knew why Freak had always wanted Ray in the review. Ray noticed how close we were. Since Ray notices everything, that wasn't a surprise. The surprise was that he volunteered to end his moment in the spotlight.

"I see our cruise is nearing tonight's port of call. Allow me the pleasure of one more tale, if I may."

Heads nodded assent.

"Consider with me, the life of Amelia Earhart. According to her Transport License, she stood only five foot and eight inches tall and weighed a scant 118 pounds. Of course, those numbers are not likely to be precise, after all who doesn't fudge a little on their driver's license?"

Emily and Jade laughed a little, taking on the roles Rachel and Bobbie Jo had performed so well back in the days when The Amazing Raymond used to mix in the occasional joke during his unmatched demonstrations of mental acuity. The scripted laughter was designed to hide the fact that he often isn't that funny, but it wasn't needed this time.

Courtney smiled and laughed. "I know I always have fudged a little." She poked me gently. "The only thing that changes with time is which way I fudge which measurement."

Raymond let her have the laugh like a consummate straight man before continuing. "Whatever Ms. Earhart's precise statistics were, I think it's safe to assume that neither her size nor her gender would have naturally led her to a career in aviation. Nevertheless, she did choose that career. I think it proved to be the right choice."

I hoped Emily or Jade would pick up the cue, because I hoped to be a spectator in this show. Emily did.

"Are you sure? Didn't I read something about her dying tragically as a result of a plane crash?"

"Indeed, I recall something about that, too. Of course, four of the five of us in this car also attended the funeral of Franz Scholes, AKA The Absolutely, Incredible Freak Show, a few years back. I spoke to him recently, and he seemed hale and hearty. Unlike Mr. Scholes, I'm sure Ms. Earhart has died by now, given that she would be over one hundred and ten years old by now."

On cue, the girls laughed, including Courtney.

"But regarding that alleged tragic ending. The evidence suggesting that an experienced pilot like herself simply crashed her plane and died is in extremely scant supply. More likely, she died as the winds of war were progressing inevitably toward the Second World War, because somebody in the Pacific Rim decided that only a female spy would be flying solo into their part of the world."

I made a note to ask Ray if he'd included the conspiracy theory for my benefit, but I never did.

Raymond continued, "Of course that theory doesn't depend on her actually being a spy, but there exists no proof that she wasn't one.

If she was a spy, then I'd say, it's safe to presume that her service to her country justified her career choice even if her end was tragic. Anybody disagree?"

Nobody disagreed, but I couldn't resist. "Perhaps when we get to the Beltway, Ms. Remington will grant us access to some of the older files at her disposal."

"She most definitely will not!" Her voice was terse, but I could see her smile out of the corner of my eye.

She turned back to face Raymond. "Nice show, Raymond. I'd been told your work with The Absolutely, Incredible Freak Show and Revue was a cover story so you could guard him. When I read your profile, I'd doubted that story until I learned how different your parlor trick was from your co-stars talents."

I didn't know how Courtney knew Raymond wasn't Rick Blaine, but I knew it probably didn't matter. If she had a problem with him being with us, she wouldn't have played along this far.

Ray said. "Now, what do you think?"

"Now, I don't care. If you prepared that whole bit, just so you could dodge my questions, you are clearly committed to the cause. That is all that matters to me."

"Is it, really? You don't care if I can shoot or fight or actually protect anybody. What if I can't?"

"Can you?"

"I can do the single most important thing a bodyguard can ever be asked to do, and if it comes to that, I will."

I don't know why, but I believed him completely. At 11:47, we passed the sign welcoming us to Olive Branch, Mississippi. I noticed that the population was 31,830. They don't call him The Amazing Raymond for nothing.

27 Changed Plans

After an uneventful Saturday night in the uneventful city of Olive Branch, Mississippi, we passed the city limits marker the next morning at 6:53 a.m. As we had starting out yesterday, Courtney rode shotgun. I sat in the back with Emily and Jade. After changing out rental cars again, we rolled through a drive thru donut shop and got five coffees; a dozen glazed and a dozen mixed.

I passed the donuts out on request as Ray guided us back on to I-30. Our seventy three mile per hour breakfast was mostly devoid of conversation. I noticed Courtney texting a couple of times, but felt no need to remark on it. We still had eight donuts left when I ran out of takers. I had just set the donuts aside when I got a text.

"Find some place private and call me, ASAP!"

I knew Letot wanted me to use some ruse to get off by myself before I called him, so I spent a minute trying to think of one that might work. I quickly remembered that I'm a terrible liar, and the only person who ever believes my lies is the man who wanted me to call him.

With that in mind, I asked Raymond to mute the stereo and clicked the call-back button on the text screen. Letot answered, promptly, curtly and tersely.

"Private! You do know the meaning of the word 'private,' don't you?"

"That is one of the words I know the meaning of, thanks for asking. That's why you're not on speaker. In case you forgot, we're on our way to thc Bcltway. I scc no reason to pull off the highway to call from some double secret phone booth. We both know I'm going to repeat every thing you tell me, anyway."

"I suppose you are, at that. Hell, I suppose you even should. The safe house you just left wasn't safe. It has been burned completely to the ground. The fire department is there now putting out the flames."

"I'm glad we got an early start this morning."

"You do realize this isn't funny, don't you."

"I know it isn't. Do you know any thing more about how it happened?"

"Not yet, but I will."

"Call me back when you find out." I hung up without waiting for a response.

Emily put her hand on my knee. "That didn't sound good. Is everything okay?"

"Not as great as it could be; the safe house we just left has been burned to the ground. We should probably proceed on the assumption that none of Letot's safe houses are going to be particularly safe."

Courtney took her eyes off her phone and looked at Raymond. "Can you get off the highway at the next exit, please?"

Raymond smiled, "Of course, I can. Is there any reason that I should?"

"Two reasons. One is that I don't think well at eighty miles per hour. The other is that there's no reason to keep driving until we know where we should go."

Raymond nodded, "Works for me." He caught my eye in the mirror. "You got any thoughts, Boss? How well do you think at high speed?"

"Not well enough. Pull over when you can and we'll regroup. This is a shock, but it's not the end of the world. The bad guys want us to be scared, and they're trying hard to make that happen."

Raymond exited the highway and pulled off into a Motel 6 parking lot. He drove to the back of the lot and pulled through two spots so we were parked facing out and ready to leave in a hurry. It's a pretty common maneuver, but I wasn't sure where Raymond had learned it. This didn't seem the time to ask, so I didn't.

Courtney was taking deep breaths, but other than that, there was no indication that we were a scared group. Maybe the bad guys hadn't tried hard enough to scare us, yet.

Jade cleared her throat. Even as I heard her do it, I didn't expect her to say anything, but I was wrong. "I don't know about the rest of you, but I'm not scared. If they burned that house to scare me, they don't know one thing about me. I spent the first fifteen years of my life watching my people burn down houses with women and children inside them. I've spent the last five years wondering every day if today would be the day that my husband looked in the wrong place for the wrong missing child and got himself killed. If these idiots think they can scare me by burning an empty house a thousand miles from Blake, they don't know one single thing about me or my life."

Jade was starting to shake, but I could tell it wasn't from fear. I'd seen that shake many times before, but seldom from anybody that small and never from Jade. Usually, I see it either just before a fight breaks out or just before Freak or Sam The Man prevents a fight from breaking out.

Today, Emily took charge. "Jade, Honey, it's okay." Emily pulled Jade into an embrace and they simply held each other while Jade regained her innate calmness. When they ended the embrace, Jade repeated, "I am not afraid."

Courtney reached back from the front seat and squeezed Jade's hand. "That's a girl." She looked at Emily. "May I borrow your husband for a few minutes? Official business, I promise."

Emily smiled, "Of course."

Courtney opened her door and stepped out. I did the same, but hesitated just long enough for her to close the door behind her. "Ray, protect these ladies with your life. If you have to take off, take off. Even if you have to run somebody over, don't hesitate, just go. We'll let Courtney and Letot explain any dead bodies you leave behind."

Raymond laughed as if he thought I was joking, but he started the car as I closed the door. I also heard him lock it as I turned toward Courtney. The morning temperature was comfortable, if slightly brisk, but Courtney shivered as she zipped her Victoria Secret Love Pink hoodie up tightly. She was walking across the parking lot back toward the front of the motel. I used my longer legs to catch up to her and put my arm around her shoulder.

She wrapped one arm around my waist and we walked slowly. "I promised your wife this was official business."

"It is. Team morale is part of official business. Are you okay? You seem pretty shook up, and we're still casualty free. You weren't expecting this to be easy, were you?"

"No, I guess not, but I thought part of it would be. I thought I could trust my people and Letot's. At least, I thought I could trust them to keep the bad guys from making a run at us in the first safe house we stayed at. What if we'd stayed there another hour? What if we'd forgotten something and went back while they were burning it down? We could all be dead now."

I shook my head. "Maybe, but I don't believe it. I still don't think we're in any danger unless and until I tell them they can't have what they want. I think they plan to keep scaring us at every opportunity until they think I'm ready to cave. I think they planned to burn that safe house only after we left in order to prove they could."

Courtney shivered again, "Do you have a plan?"

I thought about her question. "I'm still fine with the first plan, but I'm open to suggestions. Do you have any?"

"I'm not sure, but I might. Why don't you go back to the car? I need to make a few calls."

I nodded agreement. I walked to the car backing up without taking my eyes off Courtney. Whatever threat I thought I might have been guarding against never materialized. When I got in the car, Raymond and Emily were discussing the various advantages and disadvantages of various methods of bidding toward slam in the game of contract bridge.

Having played the game with Emily for years, I know she prefers the Gerber Convention of bidding four clubs, so I wasn't surprised at all by her side of the discussion. I also wasn't surprised that Raymond knew every detail of several other options. I wondered briefly if he'd ever played bridge, but quickly realized that I didn't really care.

At 9:43, when Courtney got in the car, Raymond was expounding on the Blackwood Convention method, and Jade was eating another donut. I was listening, watching, but mostly wondering what the folks who blew up the safe house would think about their plan to scare us into submission if they could see us now.

As soon as she was seated comfortably in the front passenger seat, she looked at Raymond. "So, does your human atlas include any details about beautiful Granite Falls, North Carolina?"

Whatever lack of confidence Courtney had shown earlier was gone. She was back in control and back in charge, at least back in charge of herself and her team. She'd never been in charge of the rest of us, as Raymond had made clear when he asked me if he should exit the highway. I don't think not being in charge of us bothered her near as much as it bothered Letot.

Raymond hesitated theatrically before pointing at the cars on board computer and answering, "I couldn't tell you its exact population, and I might need the GPS for directions. If I recall correctly, though, it is somewhere near Lake Hickory."

Courtney clapped. "Okay, I'm impressed. They say Granite Falls is so small and secluded that even the Governor of North Carolina doesn't know it exists, let alone where. What else do you know about Granite Falls?"

From the back seat, I interrupted. "Oh please, Raymond, let's not." I didn't know if I was saving him from having to admit to being stumped or saving me from having to hear every thing Raymond knows about Granite Falls, North Carolina. I also didn't care.

Raymond smiled, "As you wish, Boss."

I asked Courtney, "Is there anything in particular that should interest us about Granite Falls, other than the fact that Jethro Jones moved there from Virginia Beach, Virginia a couple of decades ago?"

I don't know what reaction, if any, I was hoping for or expecting from Courtney, but what I got was priceless. She spun around and looked at me as if I was smarter than Sherlock Holmes and more dangerous than Moriarty. If random feats of memory were this impressive, it's no wonder Raymond's ego had been known to get out of control on occasion.

"How in the Hell did you know that?"

28 Family History

I shrugged humbly. At least, I hoped I shrugged humbly. Shrugs tend to convey anything from petulance to disinterest without much being controllable.

"It came up in conversation a few years back. I don't have the steel trap memory that my bodyguard does, but I do occasionally remember a thing or two."

"Of course, you do. Did I tell you that?" She didn't give me time to answer, "No! I absolutely did not tell you that. Who told you about J.J.?"

"It wasn't you; not one thing I know about Jethro Jones came from you."

"How much do you know about him, and who did you learn it from?" She sounded like she expected an honest, complete answer from me. Government officials tend to be unreasonably optimistic about things like that.

I smiled, "Next question."

She resisted the urge to smile back. "Damn it, Carl. I have a right to know what you know and where you learned it. You know what I do and who I work for. There are things about the past that could directly impact national security. I have a right to know everything you know about us."

"Maybe you do, but I have the right to make a living, also. You do remember that I'm a detective, right? I make my living by asking people questions; sometimes getting answers, and never telling anybody who answered what question."

Courtney relaxed, but only a little. "And not saying anything to anybody is the part you do best. I guess I'll accept that for now because I consider you a friend, and I trust you."

"Should I be more impressed that you consider me a friend or that you trust me?"

She smiled, "Next question."

I knew she didn't want me to ask the next question. I also knew I didn't have a next question so I said nothing. As Courtney had just pointed out, not saying anything is what I do best.

Brian D. Eyre

I'd been successfully not saying anything for less than a minute when Courtney asked in a much more relaxed tone, "How much do your people know about me?"

"Jade knows only that you work for the Federal Government. Emily knows anything I know and probably some things I've forgotten. For obvious reasons, I'm reluctant to speculate about what the Amazing Ray might know, but all he learned from me is that you would be riding to the beltway with us."

"I see. Well, if my plan is going to work, I should share a couple of other little details."

She hesitated as if waiting for one of us to object, but I knew that wasn't the reason. I'd heard her tell parts of this story before. I suspect it gets a little bit easier with more time and more telling, but probably not very much easier.

"Jethro Jones is my brother. We were both born and mostly raised in a ghetto in Virginia Beach. As a teenager, he moved to North Carolina to live with his grandfather. He is now the official mayor of Granite Falls. Unofficially, he also holds every other title from dog catcher to mafia boss. I think he can provide us a safe house that is much safer than anything Letot or my department can provide."

She paused again. I knew why, but I couldn't think of anything to say that would help. I also knew that this audience would be much easier than many of her previous audiences.

She continued without prompting. "The thing is that my brother, Jethro, didn't have a sister until after he moved to North Carolina. He always thought I was his brother, Jesse, until we were both adults. Shortly before he moved to North Carolina, I moved to Baltimore. I had gender reassignment surgery there. I never intended to have contact with my family again, but I did."

I knew that her family knew much more about her orientation before she left Virginia than that from what I'd learned while investigating the Woodbury murder, but if Courtney wanted to believe or have other people believe that nobody knew anything about her until after her gender reassignment surgery was complete, I had no problem with that.

After a short silence, Courtney asked, "What? No outrage, no shock?"

132

Raymond took the bait, "Outrage or shock, over what? You found yourself stuck with a penis you didn't want, so you had it removed. What's the big deal? I had a wife once I felt that way about. I can only hope it didn't cost you as much to have your issue removed as it cost me."

When the laughter subsided, Courtney said, "Okay. I should have known that nobody in this car would have a problem with my history. The thing is, Granite Falls is not Dallas. It especially isn't Deep Ellum. J.J. is the only one there who knows anything about it, and nobody else there can ever know, period!"

"That's easy enough. You knew I wouldn't say anything. Now you know none of us will say anything. If your plan is to go to North Carolina, shouldn't we be on the highway instead of parked at a hotel?"

"Does that mean you think it's a good plan?"

"It means I'm willing to try it. If I have any questions about it, we can discuss them on the way. How far is it from here?"

Raymond couldn't resist showing off again, "Just under six hundred miles. Depending on how many times we stop because you want to change rental cars or one of the ladies need to pee; we should be able to get there by midnight or one in the morning."

I looked at Courtney who nodded. "That sounds about right. Even if it's later than that, J.J. will make sure we have an adequate welcoming committee."

Raymond started the car and took us out of the motel parking lot. My phone rang just as Raymond pulled back onto the Interstate 40. I saw it was Letot, so I answered, "Pegasus Investigations; solving crimes and destroying Government Property since 1959."

"You're in a pretty good mood for somebody who's lucky to be alive."

"I've never really believed in luck, Letot. I particularly don't believe it to be a factor in my current state of health and well-being."

Letot sighed, "It's always the lucky ones who don't believe in luck. A house you were staying in burns to the ground less than thirty minutes after you leave it. How do you explain that if luck isn't involved?"

"Clean living and a kind disposition," I suggested.

Letot snorted. "I'd bust your chops about this, but it looks like you're right. The fire appears to have been started well after you left by two men who watched you leave before they started it."

"Anybody we know?"

"Probably, but we don't have good descriptions from any of the witnesses. We'll keep at it, but don't expect us to learn too much."

"I never do, Letot. I never do."

"I'm going to let that slide, too. You have a plan?"

"Actually, we do. We plan to move Jade and Emily to a place we don't need your help guarding. That way if somebody burns it down, we'll know they didn't find them because of you."

"You're pushing it, my friend. But I suppose you've earned the right. I'll let you know what we find out. You make sure you protect those ladies."

"Of course, Letot; the main point of this part of the mission is to safeguard Emily and Jade."

"I know that, Carl. When I said protect the ladies, I meant all three of them."

He hung up without waiting for a reply. Since I had no reply to give, that didn't bother me.

29   Conveniences Store

Raymond's statement that we were less than six hundred miles from Granite Falls, North Carolina was, as expected, completely accurate. We only changed rentals three times, and we took care of other necessary business while changing, so we reached the bridge over Lake Hickory on I-321 at 11:35.

Raymond had been buried in his iPad since I took over driving at 7:30. Jade and Emily had been asleep for at least two hours. At 10:48, Courtney had pulled out her phone and started texting furiously. When she told me where to turn, she broke forty-two minutes of comfortable silence.

"The Quickie Mart will be the first brightly lit parking lot on the right when we're over the lake."

"Tell me again why we're going to The Quickie Mart?"

"Next question."

"Okay, could you maybe tell me why you have declined for five hours and seventeen minutes now to tell me why we're going to The Quickie Mart."

"Next question."

I didn't' get to ask the question I had in mind because I was pulling into The Quickie Mart and a new question immediately formed.

"Are the three guys holding UZI's with us or against us?"

"They're with us. So are the two on the roof you didn't notice."

I glanced up at the roof and saw the two guys she'd mentioned. "Is having an armed patrol good for business?"

"That always depends on what business you're in."

"Of course, it does. I don't think I'll be asking again why this had to be the first stop."

She smiled, "That's good to know."

"Do I want to know what business The Quickie Mart is in?"

"Doesn't matter, you're about to find out whether you want to know or not."

Three minutes later, Courtney and I walked into a back room of the Quickie Mart to talk with Jethro Jones. I haven't been in the back rooms of very many convenience stores, but I'm certain that the décor in this one should not be considered typical.

This room was about the size of Pegasus Investigations' lobby, but it had much nicer furniture and more deer heads mounted on the walls. I don't know if Bill Gates has a hunting lodge, but if he does, it probably looks very much like the back room of The Quickie Mart in Granite Falls, NC.

Jethro sat behind a mahogany desk that would have looked right at home in Larry Joe McCoy's law office. Courtney and I sat across from him in comfortable leather chairs. Jethro looked at me.

"My sister speaks well of your honesty and discretion. Can your associates also be trusted?"

Courtney quickly answered for me, "J.J., we already covered this. You either help all of us, or you shouldn't have offered to help."

"Sis, relax. I'm going to help you. I told ya I'd help ya, so I'm gonna help ya! I just don't know how much of our operation here can be shared with how much of his party."

"You can share it all with everybody. For Gawdsakes, J.J. I'm the agent in charge of this area. If they do say anything about your operation, it's going to end up on my desk. None of that matters, though. They aren't the type to run their mouths with no reason, and you aren't going to give them a reason, anyway."

"No, we're not." J.J. looked from Courtney to me and continued. "I trust you, which means my people trust you. Do you and your people trust me?"

"I trust Courtney, which means my people trust Courtney. She trusts you, so I guess we do. Why?"

"I'd like to borrow all of your cell phones for about thirty minutes."

I couldn't immediately think of any reason he would want them. I also couldn't think of any reason to let him borrow them. I don't know enough about cell phones to know what the risks of loaning them might be. While I was considering these things, J.J. spoke to his sister.

"Is he doing the silent act you were warning me about?"

She grinned, "Sounds to me like he is, but I'm not an expert on the Carl Jennings silent act."

I was tempted to see how long they might discuss my silent act as if I wasn't there, but I didn't bother. For one thing, it wouldn't accomplish anything. For another, I had a question to ask.

"Would it imply a lack of trust if I asked why you want all our phones and what you plan to do with them?"

He laughed. "Probably, a bit, but I won't call you on it. I'd like to reprogram them so they don't accurately reflect their locations to the satellites. Doing so will make the GPS navigators useless, but will also play Hell with any of Courtney's cohorts who might try to track you."

"Jesus Christ, is that even possible?"

Courtney answered. "It's very possible and very illegal. If you do decide to tell anybody about it, you won't just hurt my brother. You'll also cost me my job and probably put me in jail."

"I don't have a problem with letting you have my phone, and I promise that none of my people will tell anybody about your reprogramming operation. But I don't want to speak for anybody about giving up their phone." I stood, "Let me go see if anybody has a problem giving up their phone for a little while."

J.J. waved me to stay. He reached for an intercom, "Gretchen, could you invite the rest of Courtney's friends to join us in my office."

The disembodied, feminine voice from the intercom sounded as southern as Scarlett O'Hara, "Sure, I will, Boss; they'll be right in."

In just under two minutes, we were joined by Emily, Jade and Raymond. Once J.J. explained the plan, everybody agreed. As we all put our cell phones on his desk, he again reached for the intercom.

"Gretchen, please send Martin in here."

This time a male voice replied, "Be right there, Sir."

When Martin came in, I tried to decide if he'd been one of the guys holding a gun outside as we entered, but I couldn't be sure. He looked like he'd been a Marine once, but not recently. As he picked up the phones, he asked, "How you want 'em? Scrambled to Holy Hell or Hell bent to some random place?"

J.J looked at Courtney. "You call it, Sis."

She answered without batting an eye as if this was all in a day's work for her. "Travelling to the Beltway at the same pace we travelled from Dallas."

Martin smiled, "No problem, Boss Lady."

He started toward the door, but Courtney called out, "Hold on a second."

He paused, and Courtney looked at me and winked. "Carl, do you think we'll be safe here for half an hour or so without your bodyguard?"

It took me a couple of seconds to figure out where she was going. Given my reputation for slow responses, that probably worked out well.

"I guess so, why?"

"There might be some very personal information on somebody's SIM cards. I think everyone will feel more comfortable if Raymond hangs out with Martin while the phones are reprogrammed."

J.J. sighed. "Your idea of mutual trust leaves a Hell of a lot to be desired, Sis. Martin, do you mind if the little guy comes with you?"

Martin looked at Raymond briefly. "Your call, Boss, I don't care."

J.J. nodded at Raymond, "Don't ask him a bunch of questions. Martin is a technical genius and a trained killer. He is not a people person and he is not a conversationalist."

Raymond winked at Courtney as he stood up and followed Martin out the door.

As they walked out the door, I heard Raymond say, "Marty, my man, I guess we have a lot in common."

I hoped with every fiber of my being that Raymond didn't plan to follow that up by saying anything about beautiful friendships. I've never been particularly good at knowing what to hope for.

138

30   Redneck Haven

At 12:37 in the morning, the five of us piled into a Lexus SUV which J.J. produced seemingly out of nowhere. Courtney insisted on driving, which met with no resistance at all.

As she maneuvered us out of The Quickie Mart parking lot, she said, "What? No macho resistance to letting a woman drive? Are both you guys trying to change the stereotype of how men feel about letting women drive?"

Raymond answered, "Statistics show that women are five percent less likely to cause an accident than men. Why wouldn't we want you to drive?"

"Then why didn't you ask the ladies to drive from the time we left Dallas?"

"Because women are also eleven percent more likely to get lost than men. We trust that you know the way from here."

Coutney laughed, "If I don't, we're all screwed. We are on our way to a part of the world that isn't on any map. Buckle up tight and hold on to your hats."

I know better than to question any of Raymond's facts, but I suspect that if women truly are less likely to cause an accident than men, it's because women generally drive less aggressively than men. Courtney drove much more aggressively than most men, but she successfully got us to our destination without an accident.

At 1:43, she parked the Lexus in a garage in a plantation style house which I can best describe as being about an hour away from Granite Falls, NC, but in an otherwise completely indeterminate location. She closed the garage door behind us before she cut the engine.

As we entered, Raymond asked, "Did all plantations come with attached four car garages? I don't remember reading that in American History."

Courtney answered, "If you don't remember it, then I'm sure they didn't. I'm also sure that all plantations didn't come with most of the other features in this house. Let's just say the current owner bought it as a fixer upper."

Jade whistled, "Then, the current owner should be in the fixing up business. This place is amazing."

Emily nodded in agreement. "It's definitely nice, but how long are we expecting to stay here?"

Courtney answered, "I'm not sure, maybe a day or two. I don't want us to move until we're sure we have a safe place to go. I've got people working on that; people I still trust."

I suggested, "By which you mean people who aren't Maurice Letot."

"Actually, I still trust Letot, at least as much as I ever did. Unfortunately, some of the people he's trusted over the years may not be on his side on this one. Until we know for sure, I'd rather not rely on them if we can help it."

Jade asked a question I know had been on her mind for hours.

"If the safe houses aren't even safe, how can we expect the government to keep the rest of the country safe?"

Courtney stared at her for three full seconds before answering.

"Maybe, you can't. Maybe, there's no such thing as safe. The point is to try to be as careful as possible. A safe house is only as safe as the situation allows it to be."

She paused before continuing.

"Take Carl's fortress. It's about as a safe as a house can be. I know that at times, people have tried to blow it up and burn it down without success. Are there any other incidents that escaped my attention, Carl?"

"Next question."

"Of course, my point is that Perlini built a pretty safe house. But, the sixty-four thousand dollar question is how safe would it be from the guy who built it. If Perlini wanted to breach it, could he?"

Nobody answered, so she looked directly at me. "Seriously, Carl, if it were Perlini instead of his former mercenaries trying to breach your fortress, do you think he could?"

"He probably could, but if he did, he'd be a dead man walking. Don't forget, I put a couple of my best people in charge of guarding our impenetrable fortress. I didn't do that just to give them something to do. I did it because I'm not completely sure Perlini isn't trying to take his fortress back."

Raymond laughed, "You're also not completely sure that The Long Kiss Goodnight wasn't based on actual events."

"When you get a minute, feel free to look up Operation Northwoods, and tell me if you're sure it wasn't."

"I don't need to look it up. 1962's Operation Northwoods validates you and your mentor's Kennedy theories more than it suggests anything in Renny Harlin's 1996 film."

Courtney asked, "Dare I ask about your Kennedy theory?"

I smiled, "Only if you're willing to show me all the files."

"What files? I can get you a copy of the Warren Commision Report if you want it."

"No thanks. When I read fiction, I like to read fiction that's labeled as fiction. That's one reason I try not to read our local newspaper if I can avoid it."

"Of course, you do. My agency operates on the theory that private operators would rather create fiction than to read it."

I didn't respond, and nobody else commented. It had been a long day, and we were all ready to turn in. Courtney told us breakfast would be served at nine-thirty as she led us upstairs and showed us all to our rooms.

The room she gave to Emily and me would have worked as the honeymoon suite of any five-star hotel. I wondered if she'd given us this room knowing that or if all the rooms in the house were just as nice.

"I told you if you married me, we'd travel the world staying in the finest of places."

"No, you didn't, Escamillo. You told me you'd leave your beloved home state one time so I could enjoy a two-week cruise before settling into a hermit-like existence as the wife of a seventh generation Texan."

"Well, I almost kept that promise. I'm sorry you didn't get the full two weeks."

"It's all right, my darling. I blame that on your business partner and his flare for the dramatic, not on you. Do you think we can celebrate our honeymoon again tonight and still make it downstairs for breakfast tomorrow morning?"

31   Cellular Technology

We could and we did. Since Emily is never on time for anything, I considered it a major accomplishment that we made it downstairs at 9:48. When we arrived, Courtney was the only one in the dining room.

She smiled when she saw us, "This morning, it dawned on me that normal people actually sleep more than a few hours a night, so I set up a little buffet in the kitchen so breakfast will be served all morning."

"That's probably true of normal people, I'm a little bit surprised Raymond isn't here yet, though?"

"Oh, he came down about 7:15. He and Martin went on an errand for J.J. He didn't tell you he was doing it? I assumed he had. What kind of bodyguard leaves the body he's guarding without telling him?"

"What kind of Government Agent makes assumptions about how a private detective's bodyguard should operate?"

"Touche! Besides, we all know he's not really your bodyguard."

Several responses came to mind, but I decided to keep them to myself. I expected if I let that slide, she'd let it slide, as well. I was right.

She continued without a reply from me, "Anyway, Raymond and Martin should be back in a few hours. I've known Martin for years, and I've never seen him ask for help or even accept help from anybody. Apparently, Raymond isn't just amazing for his memory."

I gave that some thought. Raymond's always been famous for not being a people person, and Martin hadn't been described as a people person either. Maybe, there's some bond that forms instantly when somebody who doesn't like people meets somebody else who doesn't like people.

Of course, it's also possible that one or both of them were faking it to get something from the other. I couldn't think of anything Martin might have that Raymond might want, and I was pretty sure anything Martin might get from Raymond wouldn't negatively impact us or our mission, so I turned my attention to more important things.

"I think I can take care of myself until my bodyguard returns. Where's this breakfast you promised."

Courtney shook her head, but she led us into the kitchen where the breakfast buffet was set up.

I suspect Emily might have preferred the more diverse brunch buffet that Sapristi in Fort Worth offers, but the biscuits and gravy, bacon, scrambled eggs and pancakes that Courtney had set out suited me just fine. If Emily had any complaints, she politely kept them to herself.

The three of us ate breakfast and made small talk as if it was just another peaceful morning on a plantation in the middle of nowhere. It clearly wasn't just another peaceful morning, but I was busy enjoying my breakfast, so I didn't mind.

At 10:27, Jade joined us in the dining room. As always, she looked beautiful and tiny, but for one of the few times I could remember, she also looked tired.

Emily asked, "How you holding up, Jade?"

"I'm okay, just not used to sleeping without Blake beside me."

After everybody had eaten breakfast, Courtney offered a tour of the house. I accepted immediately, but Emily and Jade both declined. The house, and its security features, impressed me every bit as much as Courtney had suggested they would.

From the command center, we saw Emily and Jade on the monitor chatting in one of the sitting rooms. As I watched them, I began to wonder why they had declined to join the tour.

Courtney must have read my mind.

"I don't think your wife believes Jade is as tough as she's trying to act."

"Maybe. Or maybe they're discussing Parcheesi strategy."

"You're not even a little worried about her emotional state?"

"I'm not. For such a small girl, she's a big girl. She'll be fine. If there is a problem, it's above my pay grade. Emily or Blake will have to handle it."

We finished the tour of the house with no more discussion of Jade's emotional condition. At 1:52, we were back in the living room, and I heard the sound of a garage door opening. I looked my question at Courtney, and she answered, "Probably Martin and Raymond, nothing to worry about."

I kept my doubts that Martin was nothing to worry about to myself. The idea was that we were all allies that trusted each other. In that spirit, I tried to not be noticed as I put my hand in the pocket where my pistol rested.

As we watched Martin and Raymond walking down the hall toward the living room, I sensed that Courtney was even more nervous than I was. As soon as they got close enough, I also noticed that Raymond looked more pleased with himself than I'd ever seen him look, which is saying something given that he is almost continually pleased with himself."

In a shriek that sounded like some women sound when they answer yes to a long awaited marriage proposal, Courtney asked, "Did it work?"

Martin nodded casually. "Yes, Ma'am, it worked. I couldn't have done it without this little genius, but it worked."

Courtney shrieked again and rushed toward Martin and hugged him."

I looked at Raymond. "Should I ask what worked?"

Raymond blushed slightly. "Yes, but Marty should tell you."

After Courtney and Martin had hugged, she, Raymond and Martin exchanged a few high fives.

I waited patiently. Finally Martin said, "Boss, your ability to say nothing is amazing. Most people would be begging to know what it is we're so proud about."

I nodded silently, wondering if I was even interested in what achievement had caused Martin and the Amazing Raymond to be so proud. I got my answer quickly.

"We know where April is being held."

"Great! Let's go."

"Easy there, Boss. It's not quite that simple."

I'm not sure why Martin was calling me boss, maybe he calls everybody boss. I do know that I didn't expect any aspect of this project to be simple.

Courtney said, "Martin, maybe you should walk Carl through the steps you took and what you learned."

"Sure, Boss Lady."

He looked at me, "I don't need to remind you that everything we did is probably illegal in many ways. Using the GPS data from your phone and Raymond's incredible memory, we were able to get the same information from your business partner's phone."

I asked, "Exactly how did you do that?"

Courtney answered, "Let's not go for exactly, Martin. I think Carl would be happier with an overview."

"Okay, we traced your cell phone location to a time when you were with Freak and Raymond. From there we accessed a database, never mind whose database, of phone data to pick up his identifiers. Repeating that process eventually led us to April's phone and the people who kidnapped her."

He paused. I resisted the urge to show him that I was both in awe and terror at the very idea that this was even possible.

He continued. "We made the assumption that one of the first things the kidnappers would do would be to completely disable her phone. Her phone quit broadcasting three minutes after she was kidnapped. Its last location was at the entrance to the west bound entrance on Interstate 30 near Ervay in Dallas."

"If it got shut down that quick, how sure can you be that you know where she is now?"

"We used the same backtracking technique to find the phones that were closest to her when it got shut down. We got enough to be sure. One of the phones belonged to and was still with the kidnapper who died."

"Okay, I believe you. Why can't we go get her?"

Raymond answered my question for Martin with a question for me. "How much do you know about Palo Duro Canyon?"

"I know it's the second largest canyon in the United States and that it's pretty close to Amarillo in the Texas Panhandle."

"Do you know how many caves are in it?"

I suspected this was just Raymond angling for another chance to show off, but I presumed it was at least slightly relevant, so I played along.

"I'll bite; how many caves are there in Palo Dura Canyon?"

"I don't know either." Raymond admitted, which was probably harder for him than for most people. "Martin, why don't you explain the rest?"

"Caves play Hell with cell phone tracking. But at least one of the two phones that were with April in downtown Dallas when she was kidnapped has been in that canyon constantly. The problem is that we can't track it close enough to know exactly where."

Raymond looked at me, "As you said, it's the second biggest canyon in the country."

I asked, "So what do we do?"

Courtney answered, "I think we should do what we started out to do. Let's go to D.C., get the girls safely tucked away and see what the Pentagon files tell us about the douche bags that took April."

"Do you have a safe house arranged?"

"I do."

"Is it as nice as this one?

She smiled. "No, it isn't. But it's a Hell of a lot bigger and is probably the second most secure building in the world.

Raymond said, "Big enough to have two hundred and eighty four bathrooms, I bet."

"I've never counted, but that's probably about right."

I expected Raymond was about to start impressing Martin and Courtney with encyclopedic knowledge of the Pentagon, so I quietly slipped into another room to make a phone call. I almost never look forward to making phone calls, but this call to Freak was a clear exception.

Telling Freak that we knew where April was being held wouldn't be as nice as it would be if I could tell him that we had her out safe, but it would be close. Freak answered on the third ring.

"What's up, Boss? I trust you're calling with good news."

"I'm not your boss, but I am calling with good news. We think we know where April's being held. Is your army assembled and ready to march into battle?"

He answered with so much confidence, that I started looking forward to hearing every detail of how he and his army rescued the damsel in distress. Looking forward to things I end up not wanting is just one of my annoying tendencies.

Part 7 – Harsh Measures

"My defense is of God,
Which saveth the upright in heart.
God judgeth the righteous,
And God is angry with the wicked every day.

His mischief shall return upon his own head,
And his violent dealing shall come down."

David
Psalm 7

32 Twenty Questions

I awoke with a start after another dreamless sleep. A girl who's had as many nightmare-filled nights as I've had could get used to that. The only problem with it is that I keep waking up to a real nightmare. As my boss often says, irony can be so ironic.

Nothing had changed. I was still bound on a table in a bright room with a view of white walls and reddish floor. I had no idea where I was or how long I'd been there. Other than that, I seemed to be okay physically. As far as I could tell, I was okay mentally, but I've spent enough time in therapy to know that people aren't often qualified to judge their own mental state.

"Good morning, Doll Face." The voice coming from behind me had no trace of a Russian accent, so I assumed it was Cliff Parsons.

"Don't call me Doll Face." I still didn't mind the name, but I felt it important to stay in character.

"Yes, you've mentioned that you don't like being called that once or twice. The thing is I don't think I care any longer what you do or do not like. I've been nice to you in the hopes that you would be nice to me."

I remembered that he'd been asking questions of me. I was fairly certain I hadn't answered any of them to his satisfaction. I had every intention of continuing to not answer questions to his satisfaction.

"Maybe I don't really consider kidnapping me, ruining a beautiful and expensive blouse and keeping me as a hostage to be a good way of being nice to me."

He laughed. "I'll grant you that those things might make you not like me. But you have to admit, I've treated you well since you've been here. Besides, I didn't rip your blouse; that was one of my less urbane associates. On his behalf, I apologize."

He was still standing out of my view. He seemed to think that gave him some kind of advantage. I would have thought having me tied up and barely dressed would have been enough advantage, but I'm not an expert on hostage strategy.

Brian D. Eyre

"You apologize? As in, 'We're very sorry, Mrs. Kennedy. Other than that, how was your stay in Dallas?' I'm not impressed."

"No, you aren't. I've never met anybody so difficult to impress in my life. But, I promise you, we have ways to impress you. You won't like them. In fact, I don't care for them, either. That's one reason I've been patient with you, but my patience is at an end. Let's play twenty questions one more time and see if we can avoid an ending we will both dislike."

It wasn't a question, so I didn't answer it. I was already certain that Freak was going to make sure that Cliff wasn't going to like the ending. Even if they killed Freak, if that's even possible, he and Carl have too many crazy friends and crazier connections to let this guy do something bad to me and like how his story ends. The rest of my thoughts might be mush, but on this point I was clear and certain.

I heard the table scraping on the ground before I realized he was spinning me away from my view of the white walls. Once he had the table where he wanted it, I saw that the reddish walls I could now see weren't exactly an improvement over the white walls I'd been seeing before. The biggest difference is that I can see him now, which he must have thought would be to his advantage.

He sat on a barstool, so I had to look up to see his face. That's probably what he thought was going to give him the advantage. I'm five foot seven; I've been looking up at men without looking up to them for most of my life. I felt confident I'd be ready to handle that advantage of his.

"Okay, Doll Face, Tell me what you know about the Pegasus Investigations' office."

"We've been over this, Cliff. I told you what I know. I work at that office. I didn't build it."

"We have been over it, but you have been lying. I can tell when people are lying. You will tell me the truth. I'm just hoping you'll do it without getting hurt too badly."

I wasn't too worried about his alleged power to tell when people are lying since he still believed the first lie I'd told him. The getting hurt badly part scared me some, but my character's script called for me not to show that.

"Maybe you should hurt me. It might be less tedious than being asked the same questions over and over. I hear some people really get a kick out of being hurt. I might have a fetish for it that I never realized."

"It seems unlikely. You're a young lady, but you're old enough to know by now what you get your kicks from. Besides, the ways we've been trained to hurt people aren't fun for anybody."

I noticed with relief that he made no mention of my friend Rachel or her boss. The less these bastards knew about Freak's circle of friends, the more likely they would be unprepared for whatever Freak came up with to get me out of here.

"You're right, Doll Face. This is tedious. I'll ask these questions again when I think you're ready to tell me the truth."

He looked away from me and yelled, "Jerome!"

A man I'd seen a few times before walked into the room. He looked just like he'd looked before, like one of the stars of that reality show about rednecks making duck calls.

"Yes?" he asked.

"I think it's time to show Ms. Rose what you learned at Guantanamo Bay."

"Ain't I done been tellin' ya that fer days?"

"You have indeed been telling me that. Now I'm telling you that I agree. Have fun, I'll be back in a couple of days to see how it's going. Try to keep her sane enough to answer the questions."

Cliff Parson walked away leaving me face to face with a grinning redneck who'd apparently been begging for days to start torturing me using the techniques he'd learned at a prison camp internationally famous for it's failure to comply with the Geneva Convention rules on how captives can be interrogated.

I smiled the most confident smile I could muster as I waited to be water boarded. I think I managed it fairly well since I wasn't really sure what water boarding actually involves. I assumed it involves water and a board and some kind of torture.

As Jerome walked around behind me to prepare me for my torture, I tried not to think too much about what was coming next. I tried to remind myself that my husband was certainly looking for me. I also tried not to think about what happened to the last love of his life that Freak tried to find. I was still trying not to think about that when he came back around in front of me.

"Sugah Pie, I hope ya is ready to have ya dang mind blown da hell and back."

I hoped I was ready, but there was nothing I could have done to prepare for what came next. Life had either prepared me for the Gitmo treatment or it hadn't.

33 Guest Appearance

"Dead Soul went down like gasoline. I grabbed the bar for traction. But when it hit my gut, I was ready for some action."

I could barely make out the lyrics because of the volume of the song blasting my ears through the headphones. Freak and I have heard Long Sword Spectacular play this song pretty loud at Reno's, but not as loud as I was hearing it now.

When Jerome first started the music in my ears, I had relaxed, thinking if loud music was the torture method du jour, my life as a bartender and patron in and around Deep Ellum should have me prepared to handle it. Now I was just trying to maintain my sanity by trying to pick out the random lyric that I recognized from a band I knew.

The song ended and another loud song began. I didn't immediately recognize it, and I was still trying to place it when the music suddenly stopped. I saw Cliff Parsons come into view.

"Enjoying the music, Doll Face?"

I tried to flash my enigmatic smile. "I've heard worse."

"You have?"

"Of course, I have. I've worked at least twenty events featuring Emerald City."

"That doesn't make any sense at all, Doll Face."

I flashed my enigmatic smile again. This time I felt sure I nailed it. "Isn't that your goal?"

"No, Bitch! The goal is for you to tell me what I need to know."

I'd never heard him raise his voice until this moment. I chalked it up as a moral victory. I also reminded myself that all the moral victories in the world wouldn't change the fact that he had me tied up at the moment, and could keep me like this as long as he wanted.

He also had my gun, and probably many others, with which he could kill me at any time. Since each new round of questions had made it increasingly obvious that he wanted me to show him how to gain access to Pegasus' office, so he and his posse could wreak havoc in Downtown Dallas, I decided to also count it as a moral victory if he killed me without me telling him.

"I take it you still don't plan to tell me how the remote control runs the security at your office."

"It's not actually my plan. It's just that I don't know. I keep telling you that."

"You keep saying it, and I keep not believing it. I guess I'll let the music scramble your brains for a few more hours. But first, I'm going to give you something else to think about if your mind still works."

He paused and gave me a hard stare before continuing. Since I've seen much better hard stares, I had no trouble not reacting.

"I will get what I want, Doll Face. You interest me, but I will not let you stop me. When the music stops again, you will either tell me what I need to know, or I will give you to Jerome to play with for awhile. Trust me, if you interest him, it will not be to your advantage."

I trusted him. I'd watched Jerome look at me while I was trying not to let the loud music take my sanity. I definitely interested him, and it would definitely not be to my advantage. The music cranked up again. As I tried to remain sane by picking out lyrics, I also began thinking about how much detail about the office I could safely reveal without putting Pegasus or the city of Dallas at risk.

At some point I noticed that Cliff and Jerome were putting on their own show as they watched me endure the music. Cliff was waving my gun around insanely like Al Pacino in 'Dog Day Afternoon,' and Jerome was trying to look like the rednecks in 'Deliverance.'

I was trying to decide if they were doing that intentionally, when I saw them both react to something else. It must have been a noise that I couldn't hear, but I wished I could. Their reaction gave me hope that it was my knight in shining armor coming to slay the dragon and rescue me.

Jerome left the room, and Cliff quit waving the gun and held it steady. The fact that he now held it steady and pointed at me, might have scared most people; it gave me hope. Maybe that's because I'd gone crazy, but it gave me hope.

I looked at him with as little expression as I could muster. I took turns looking at his face, at my gun and at the floor. I thought it would be easier to look as if I wasn't interested in him, if I didn't stare too long in any one place. The fourth or fifth time I looked at the floor, I saw something that I cared very much about.

If there's an academy award for not reacting, I'd either just clinched it or the loud music had driven me completely insane. I saw my share of spiders in my time in Australia. I've seen even more than my share hanging out with my husband's best friend who just happens to be a lady who claims she can train spiders.

I have never seen anything like what I saw on that floor. I looked back at the gun and decided not to look at the floor again. As I continued to no longer look at the floor, I tried to remember what the spider had looked like. It was huge, even huger than the tarantulas Bobbie Jo loves likes pets.

It was also scary looking. Some people say all spiders look scary, but this thing was off the chain scary. The weirdest thing was that it seemed to have the power to shine a green light a few inches ahead of it.

I glanced back to the floor. The spider and its magical green dot were still there. The loud music had clearly driven me insane. At least I wouldn't be able to give away any secrets now. Even better, I'd never again have to listen to Emerald City.

Part 8 – Hard Wood

"You can never have the ever
In happily ever after;
Just try to smile, at least awhile
And enjoy the love and laughter.

Love can be just with one we trust,
But it can't be never-ending.
Each one of us will turn to dust;
That's the only certain ending."

The Rick Taylor Trio
"Happy Endings"

34   Travel Plans

"I'm not your boss, but I am calling with good news. We think we know where April's being held. Is your army assembled and ready to march into battle?"

I'm not sure my army had been completely assembled, but it was damn sure ready for battle. It was also way closer to being an actual army than The Great Detective had any reason to expect.

"Dude, you have no idea how assembled and ready we are. I'm actually starting to pity the fools who thought they could pull this stunt off. When I get April back, they're going to find out how bad they screwed up in a big way. Where are they holding my wife?"

He answered immediately, "About thirty miles south of Amarillo most likely in Palo Duro Canyon."

"I hear Palo Duro is a pretty big hole in the ground, would you mind maybe narrowing that down a little."

"I'd love to, but that's about all we have so far. If we get more specific details, you'll be the first person I call. You want to tell me about this army of yours?"

"I'm not sure you want to know too much about it."

I was thinking about Bobbie Jo's eight-legged soldiers when I said it, but it quickly occurred to me that he probably didn't need to know too many details about Mistress Caroline's feminist brigade or how quickly she got her hands on an impressive arsenal, either. I gave him just enough detail to give him confidence and withheld enough not to give him the creeps.

When I finished, he gave me some suggestions. Most of them I almost certainly would have thought of myself, which is probably more of a credit to the years of effort he's put into training me in this business than to any intelligence or aptitude of my own. As soon as we ended the call, I started on the one suggestion that most likely would not have occurred to me.

Naturally, it was the most important of the suggestions. I called Larry Joe McCoy's office to confirm that he was there and available before walking to Thanksgiving Tower to ask him for his help. McCoy is the most famous and/or infamous defense attorney in Dallas County. He is also my Godfather.

Since the man has known me since before I was born and gave me one of his kidneys when I needed it, I wasn't worried about what his answer would be. I just didn't think this was the kind of favor one asks for over the phone.

When I entered his lobby, Ramona smiled and pointed to the open door of his office. "Go on in. He's expecting you."

"And how many potential clients did he have you send away this time, so he could help his poor ole son?"

"We always lose count, but if he tries to blame you for more than twenty, you should assume he's lying."

"My Pops never lies. He simply expands the definition of truth to fit his needs."

She smiled radiantly. She always has a great smile, but when her smile radiates, it always means the same thing. I closed the door behind me and sat in one of Larry Joe's client chairs.

"Have you met Ramona's new beau?"

"Not yet, Pardner, but she has sure enough taken a shine to the young feller. She cain't hardly get her work done from up on that cloud she's been awalkin' on."

My godfather's cowpoke accent belies his birthplace in Upstate New York more dramatically than my wife's Texas drawl belies her birthplace in the land down under. One key difference is Larry Joe has to fake his and April's is second nature to her.

The other difference is that April doesn't tend to lose hers in times of stress like Pops does. That thought immediately took my mind off of Ramona's new love and back onto my love's current stressful situation. I wondered how she was holding up, and how long it would take for me to rescue her now that I had at least an idea about where she was being held.

Larry Joe said, "Well, Son, it looks like the silent assassin has sure enough taught you the tricks of his trade, but iffn I'm gonna be able to help y'all out, Ah reckon you ougtta tell me what y'all need."

In a way, I was glad his cowpoke accent was in full force. Usually, if he's calm, it means I should be calm. With April being held against her will seven hours away, calm wasn't exactly my mood, but I knew Larry Joe was right.

"I need places to stay near Palo Duro Canyon that cannot be traced to you, me or anybody either of us know."

"Oh, just that? For a bit thar, Ah was afeered y'all might be needin' a real favor. How big a posse will y'all need to put up in that Gawd-Forsaken place?"

As the great detective often tells me, the right question is the one that leads to the right answer. I honestly had no answer to this question, which I found somewhat embarrassing. I did what I've always done when I don't have a good answer. I fronted.

"That's not the right question, Pops. The question is how much money is in the budget for accommodating our posse."

The look on Larry Joe's face was priceless. I'm sure The Great Detective would have appreciated my comments' impact on his dialect, as well.

"Okay, Franz, I'll ask. What is your budget?"

"We are authorized to spend the full resources of Pegasus Investigations and a large majority of the annual budget of the CIA, Homeland Security and the Dallas Police Department. I also have the resources of a few more clandestine organizations about whom I'll withhold detail unless and until I ask you to represent any of their members in court."

"That, Son, is why I didn't ask about your budget. I already knew your budget was sufficient, since I keep a fairly close eye on my own bank accounts. How about this? I'll make arrangements to house about fifty people in various places in and around that area. If you need more, let Ramona know, and we'll take care of it.

That sounded like a good plan, so I agreed to it. As I left the office into the lobby, Ramona smiled again.

"When you get April back, let's all get together. I want y'all to meet Sheldon."

I kept my thoughts about her chances of a long term relationship with a man named Sheldon to myself. After all, my parents named me Franz. Besides, I'm not still not entirely sure what my wife's parents named her. I do, however, know it isn't April. I'm also reasonably certain it isn't the name the Australian authorities have on file for her either.

35   Army Rules

As I stepped out of Thanksgiving Tower, I called Osalumense. He answered on the second ring. "Greetings, my Lord. How may your liege be of assistance today?"

I resisted the urge to laugh before answering, "Many ways, not the least of which would be to quit talking like you're auditioning to be on 'Game of Thrones' next season."

He did laugh, "Consider it done. What else can I do for you?"

"Prepare for battle. We think we've found the castle where the damsel is being held. At the very least, we know where we're going to look for her."

"I thought we weren't going to talk like that."

This time I did laugh. "I didn't say I wasn't going to talk like that. I just asked you not to talk like that. Legendary Zulu Warriors like yourself should never lower themselves to talking like an extra in a Monty Python skit."

"I don't even know what a Zulu is, but I'm ready to be a warrior. Where are we going and when do we go?"

"We go west, and we leave when the accommodations are arranged for us. Can you make sure Spicoli, Rachel and Mistress Caroline all know the game is afoot and are ready to roll?"

"I can and I will. But, if you're going to keep switching your dialect from Monty Python to Sherlock Holmes, I reserve the right to go back to talking like the Knights of the Round Table."

I quickly agreed to his terms, and made my next call.

Bobbie Jo answered on the third ring, "What's up, Freak? Is the game afoot?"

I saw almost no reason to suggest that my friends don't call me Freak and even less reason to question her use of Sherlock Holmes' catchphrase.

I simply answered, "Yes. Are your troops up for a seven hour drive?"

Bobbie Jo was slow to answer, which is not her nature. I waited her out as best I could. After a long silence, I nudged. "B.J.?"

"The troops are ready, but I'm not. Charlie Ray took his tour bus to a music festival in Colorado. My lovelies can't travel in just any climate."

"Can't we rent something that will work? I can afford pretty much anything it would take."

"Freak, we've been over this before. I'm not a charity case."

Bobbie Jo Nottingham, despite having a name that sounded like British nobility, came from a long line of hard working people who have struggled to make a living going back at least to the Great Depression. Like many hard-working poor people, pride is ingrained in every fiber of her being.

She also has many more affluent friends, myself included, who would be happy to make life easier for her, if her pride would let her accept. I have many times tried deception in order to convince her to accept help. On rare occasions, I've even succeeded. Fortunately, I knew I wasn't going to have to resort to deception this time.

I told her the truth. "Bobbie Jo, I'm not offering charity. I put together an army to rescue April. It may be a volunteer army, but even volunteer armies get expenses covered. Do you know where to rent a suitable vehicle?"

"One of those RV places on Forest Lane should have something. How long will we need it, and what can we afford?"

I spared her the speech I'd given Larry Joe. Instead, I told her that we could afford any rental, and to get it for a month. After we'd worked out the details, she sounded hesitant to hang up. I knew she wasn't scared about the upcoming battle, but I could tell something was on her mind.

"Bobbie Jo, I'm just guessing here, but is there something else on your mind that I should know about?"

She sighed, "Yes. Thanks for asking. Mandy wants to come with us."

"Why is that a problem? She's almost as good with your little soldiers as you."

"The problem is I don't want her to come. If she's there, I'll be more worried about protecting her than I am about rescuing April. The mission is to rescue April."

I quickly understood the issue. It took me a little bit longer to figure out how to handle it. I was still considering options when Bobbie Joe said, "Freak, this may not be the best time for the silent act you learned from your partner."

"Sorry. I was just reviewing the Rescue April Army field guidebook, and it clearly states that wives, husbands, boyfriends and girlfriends of Arachnid Generals may not accompany the Arachnid General into battle. I'm sorry; Bobbie Jo, but rules are rules. Do you want to tell Mandy she can't come or should I do it?"

"You should. Call her now. Please come up with a better reason than that before you do."

I promised her that I would, but I probably didn't. It made no difference. When I called Mandy, it quickly became apparent that her interest in going was based more on her desire to not let Bobbie Jo think she was scared, than an actual desire to participate in a war with ruthless terrorists.

With that settled, I called Larry Joe. Ramona put me right through to him.

"Pardner, I ain't made your arrangements, yet. Even the best cookie needs a minute or two to set up camp and fire up the beans, y'know."

"That's alright, Daddy-O, I just wanted to put in a special request. At least one battalion will be travelling in an RV, so they'll need to hook up in the area."

"That's a good plan, I should have thought of it. I'll see if I can arrange for two or three spots. Do you have the vehicles or do I need to rent them?"

"Bobbie Jo is renting one. She'll be calling your office to arrange the payment when she finds one that will work."

"I take it that battalion will include some eight-legged passengers?"

"But, of course. We're going to Palo Duro Canyon to find April and rescue her from international mercenaries. Why wouldn't we bring some soldiers they might not be used to fighting?"

"Well, for one thing, tarantulas aren't actually fighters and are pretty much harmless."

"That's two things, Daddy-O, and I already knew both of them. Make the arrangements, please. If you get a spare minute, you can research banana spiders."

"Consider it done. I trust once you get April back, you'll quit bossing your Godfather around like you would a clumsy chambermaid?"

I resisted the urge to tell him that I would never boss around a clumsy chambermaid. It's much more fun to boss around wealthy, infamous defense attorneys. Besides, I don't expect to ever have a chambermaid.

Instead, I said. "Let's just get April back. That's all I'm worried about at the moment."

"Son, I don't often speak well of you when you're listening, because your ego is not one that ever needs stroked, but I'll make an exception. I would bet everything I own and everything I'll ever earn on you in this quest. I know you are going to get April back. My only concern is whether you or one of your people will do anything in the process that even I can't keep them out of jail for doing."

"Ironically, that's the one thing I don't care about at all."

36   Native Intelligence

Osalumense picked me up at my house at eight-fifteen. As I climbed into his truck, I said. "Thanks for the early morning pick-up. I know you're not a morning person."

"We Zulu Warriors do not concern ourselves with time. We are concerned only with defending Isandlwana from the British Invasion."

"I thought you said you'd never heard of a Zulu Warrior?"

"I did, didn't I? Raymond doesn't have a patent on looking up useless information on the internet, and you don't have to be amazing to remember one fact for a day or two."

Traffic on the Dallas North Tollway from the city toward the 'burbs in the morning is typically pretty light. Today was no exception. Just before nine, we parked beside Rachel's little sports car.

Rachel met us at the door, looking very pleased about something. It's a look I got very used to seeing back in the day. Today, that look was a pleasant surprise. I politely left it to her husband to ask about it.

"Baby, I hope I'm going to like what you're glowing about as much as you do."

"I'm not glowing. I'm glistening from my hard work training."

She may or may not have been glowing or glistening, but she was definitely beaming.

I don't know how many times we've shared the stage or how many times she's set up another performer with the perfect straight line, but I knew it was my turn to set her up.

"What kind of training?" I asked feeling sure that was the line she was looking for.

It was, and she nailed it. She did the complete Bill Murray spin from Stripes and said. "Army Training, Sir!"

As she did it, it occurred to me that her husband might not have even seen the movie. Rachel has taken many cross country trips with me and my collection of old movies, but he hasn't.

Either way, he applauded enthusiastically.

Rachel still beamed, "Follow me, y'all have to see this."

We followed her into the temporarily rechristened training room. Several women I didn't recognize were shooting at the hanging dummies. Spicoli was either showing off or practicing by climbing around the ceiling on the various devices that had been attached there to somehow help the clientele best live out their legal, harmless and perfectly normal fantasies.

Rachel stood between two of the women shooting at dummies. She set her purse on the ground by her feet, and pulled out a purple Crown Royal bag. I knew that neither she, nor her husband, drank expensive whiskey, so I was curious about the contents of the bag. My curiosity was satisfied quickly.

By the time I realized what she'd pulled out of the bag, she had flipped her wrist three times and the dummy in front of her was dotted by three Japanese throwing stars. She repeated the movement quickly and the dummy was soon a patchwork of stars that spelled out the letter 'R'.

Osalumense asked, "How did you learn to do that in a few days?"

"I didn't learn it. I relearned it. Before I took a boring job whipping Freak on stage with a bullwhip, I was hoping to join the circus and pin victims to a board with my shurikens."

"Aren't those shows faked?"

"Some people think so, Freak, but some people think your shows were faked, too. It doesn't really matter. I was twelve, how was I supposed to know if they were faked or not?

"I see your point." I pointed at the dummy. "That was not faked. I'm glad to know we're prepared for the enemy if they bring a ninja with a flying sword to our gun fight."

I nodded toward the room where Mistress Caroline had showed me her arsenal earlier. "We may not need it, but I'm still impressed."

"True, we could probably blow up Palo Duro Canyon if it will get April back. But if we need a silent flying sword, I'll be ready to deliver." She turned to her husband, "You're impressed, right?"

Osalumense nodded, "Of course, I'm impressed, and awed, and several other words that I don't know how to say in English."

Rachel blushed, gave him a quick kiss, and then turned to me. "Come with me. Caroline has somebody she wants you to meet."

She steered me to a corner of the large room, where Mistress Caroline was talking with a slightly built woman with matted gray hair. Gray hair doesn't always mean advanced age, but it is suggestive, and the woman's dark weathered face confirmed that she'd been on this earth for some time.

Mistress Caroline smiled when she saw us. If it was meant to be a warm smile, she still needed to work on that. She did manage to sound friendly, "Ah, there's our fearless leader. Thank you, Rachel."

Rachel left like a soldier who has been dismissed by a superior officer, which in truth, she probably was.

"Freak, I'd like you to meet Autumn Quake Hearer. Autumn, this is Freak. It is his wife we will be serving in this quest."

Mistress Caroline had accepted my command of her feminist army based on our mutually agreed agenda of rescuing April. I thought it wise not to imperil the faith Mistress Caroline had shown me regarding gender equality by suggesting an age based bias.

I extended a hand, "Delighted to meet you, Ms. Quake Hearer. My wife and I are grateful for your help; in fact all of us appreciate it."

Her handshake was surprisingly firm, yet cold and noticeably quick. She looked at Mistress Caroline. "The young man is as you described. I was wrong to doubt your judgment. I shall try not to repeat the mistake."

Turning back to me, she continued. "You may call me Autumn."

I quickly realized I had passed an audition that I hadn't even known was an audition. That recognition did not immediately suggest a logical comment, so in keeping with The Great Detective's training, I said nothing.

Caroline smiled, warmly this time, "Autumn did not believe you would accept her into our army without seeing proof that she could be of help. She said that men are usually dismissive of women, and youth is always contemptuous of the aged."

I smiled at Autumn. "You are probably correct on both counts. I have the advantage of being acquainted with Mistress Caroline. No man could be fool enough to know her and still harbor a dismissive attitude toward women."

Autumn nodded. "That might be true. Does my age also not matter to you?"

"I do not know how many years you have lived; nor do I know how many you have left. I know exactly how many years I have lived, but not how many I have left. If we both survive the coming battles, I would bet that you will have more years left than I. If we do not survive, it will not matter."

She smiled, "Well said, young man. Do you have Kiowa blood or other Indian blood?"

"Not that I know about. I'm told, though, that I had ancestors at Masada, and I know that my business partner had ancestors at the Alamo."

"Indeed? That would explain much. Few people have inherited the understanding of the Kiowa/Comanche experience. How are you more certain of your partner's ancestry than your own?"

"Carl Jenning's lineage is a matter of public record. He takes just enough pride in it to have mentioned it on occasion, and it is not in his nature to lie about such things. My family tree is somewhat murkier. As you know, youth is not known for its respect of history, and very few in my lineage have lived long past youth's embrace."

Autumn looked at Mistress Caroline, "His partner is the Carl Jennings? You should have told me. That Jennings line has been known for keeping promises for at least as long as the Kiowa and Comanche tribes have traded with white men in the Southern Plains."

Mistress Caroline shrugged without comment.

Autumn turned to me. "You have not asked how I plan to help your cause. Would you like to hear?"

I said I would, and Mistress Caroline led us to a small room that I'd never seen before. The three of us sat in comfortable chairs around an ornate glass table. I didn't know exactly how to restart the conversation, but it didn't matter. Autumn needed no prompting.

"That land belongs to the Kiowa. It belongs to us as surely as a baby girl belongs to her mother. Your government and the business men who run your government can claim the deeds and the titles, but the land belongs to us."

It was apparent that Autumn Quake Hearer had an agenda, but I saw no reason not to hear her out. After all, our army was being trained. The Great Detective had found the battle site. Larry Joe was preparing the site for the arrival of our army. As much as I wanted to rescue April sooner than later, I didn't feel that I was wasting time.

She continued, "It has always been a simple thing to own something. It is more simple now than ever. Once, you needed to trade something you own in order to own something else. Later, you could own it by trading paper for it. Now, you can promise future paper and own it. Your politicians encourage these false ideas because it makes them think they own things which are not theirs to own."

Carl would have loved her cynicism regarding the government. I hoped we all lived long enough for them to discuss it at length. If Autumn Quake Hearer was waiting for me to say something, I failed her.

"My people do not accept these rules, but we accept that they are your rules. The canyon where your wife is being held has been under attack for years. Our council has pled with your government to stop the attack, but they deny the facts."

I asked "What do you mean by under attack?"

Mistress Caroline interrupted. "Autumn, you should tell him the truth, he will understand."

"I said I would trust your judgment about him. I will keep that promise."

She turned toward me. "The Kiowa people, like those of most tribes, generally earn their names around puberty. My name was given to me when I was only seven years old. Even though I was too young to know what a tremor was, I could predict them."

I whistled, "Impressive trick for a seven year old."

"Actually, I could always do it. It was only after I turned seven that I talked about it to the elders. Until then, I never knew that other people could not hear the earth speak the way I did."

I asked, "The earth or the seismic disturbances that affect it?"

She smiled, "The earth, itself. As an infant, I only noticed when I heard the tremors, but as I matured, I heard it more often and more clearly. It speaks to me now as clearly as you and I are speaking."

I resisted the urge to suggest that she tell the earth to let us know where April was being held, but it was tempting. Instead, I tried to prove Mistress Caroline was right about me by understanding.

"It is the nature of Governments to deny those facts which do not serve their agendas. The government you call mine is no exception. What facts does it deny that relate to an attack on Palo Duro Canyon?"

"Parts of the canyon have been attacked from within itself for at least ten years. It does not happen every day, or even every week. But, it has happened, more than once. It is not acceptable. It is also unacceptable that your government refuses to admit responsibility"

I had no choice, but to admit that I didn't understand. "How is land attacked from within?"

"That is what I'm hoping you will find out."

"That's why you are helping us? You hope we can find out what the government is doing to your land."

The old lady looked at me reproachfully. Because of my circumstance, I've never had an opportunity to disappoint a grandparent, but I think I learned in that moment, what it feels like.

She said, "I am helping because an innocent woman is in peril. If we can somehow stop the damage that is being done to that canyon as we save her, then we will know the Spirits have smiled on our effort."

37　Shiny Toys

"It's all arranged Pardner, mosey on down to my office and Ramona will give you the details."

"How late will she be there?"

"I reckon she'll be here right up until she gives you the details. Even with the new beau, she still ain't the type to turn down overtime. How late you reckon it'll be?"

"Let me rephrase the question. What time does she normally leave."

Larry Joe told me that Ramona usually left at five, so I told him to let her know we'd be there by four-thirty. Osalumense and I spent a couple hours with Mistress Caroline discussing the logistics of getting her army and mine to Palo Duro Canyon and an hour and half firing various rifles and pistols at suspended dummies. Surprisingly, I even hit some of them.

At three-thirty, it was time to head downtown. Sam The Man went to find Rachel, and I went to tell Mistress Caroline we were leaving. She was in her office sitting behind her desk.

I just barely walked in to the office. "I wanted to let you know Sam and I are heading out. See you tomorrow night in Palo Duro."

"You can count on it. Have a seat, I have something for you."

I did as she asked. She reached into a desk drawer and pulled out a box and set it on the desk.

"Open it."

I did as she wished. Inside the box was a silver pistol, a holster and twenty-four bullets. I presumed the bullets would fit in the gun and the gun would fit in the holster.

After I'd had time to survey the contents, Mistress Caroline spoke, "That is a stainless steel Colt .45. It's an exact duplicate of the black one you were actually shooting accurately with in the playroom. It just looks way cooler. I want you to have it."

"You mean borrow it? We're returning the arsenal after we win, right?"

"This gun isn't from the arsenal we borrowed. It belonged to the one decent man I knew as a child. I think it should belong to a decent man again."

I was impressed when she said it, and even more so, when I noticed her eyes watering. This was a side of Mistress Caroline that I suspect few people will ever see. It was very disconcerting to me to see it, but somehow I also felt honored.

The last thing I wanted to do was discuss the one good man little Caroline, if that was her name when she was little, ever knew. With that in mind, I asked, "Should I call it Rosebud or Excalibur?"

Her face returned to its normal state which despite its hardness comforted me.

"Take the gun, Freak. I'll sleep better knowing you have a gun you might actually shoot straight when the time comes."

"So will I. Thank you, Mistress Caroline."

I picked up the box and stood up. As I did, I saw the hint of a smile appear on her lips.

"Call it Excalibur! After all, you did extract it from a stone... a stone cold bitch."

An hour later, I was in Larry Joe's office going over our accommodations with Ramona. We had 5 cabins on the rim of the canyon. We also had a handful of hotel and motel rooms in the area. These were registered under aliases that had never been used before either by Pegasus or Secure Investigations. Matching I.D.s were in the safe at our office.

Additionally, we had spots for two RV's at the canyon and two more a few miles away from the canyon at an RV park that guaranteed uninterrupted cell phone service and wifi connectivity. Our arsenal and Bobbie Jo's menagerie would be in separate RV's parked at the canyon. Our intelligence operations would be stationed in one of the RV's where the wifi and cell phone service were guaranteed.

As I was trying to work out the rest of the accommodations, Carl called. "What's up, Boss?"

I always call him 'Boss' when he calls my cell phone. Usually, he pretends that it bothers him. This time he didn't bother.

"Has any of your army started west, yet?"

"I don't think so. Please tell me you haven't lost April?"

"No, she's still there. At least, if she was ever there, she still is. We almost made a huge mistake. Raymond's on a plane heading to

Love Field. Don't let anybody head west until he gets to talk to them. You'll need to have him picked up as well; he should be at the east terminal at 6:10. Can you do that?"

"Sure, Boss. Picking him up isn't a problem...."

He sensed my hesitancy and responded much quicker than he sometimes responds to simple, direct questions.

"But, there is a problem?"

I answered vaguely, "Not all of our army will be deploying from Dallas, and not all of it speaks English." I carefully avoided any mention of the eight legged soldiers who don't speak any language no matter what my friend, Bobbie Jo might like to suggest.

"Jesus Christ, Freak, how big is this army of yours?"

"I hope it's big enough to get April back. Maybe, if we're lucky, it will also be big enough to protect our office and keep America safe for democracy."

"Right, that's okay. Raymond really doesn't need to see everybody. Make sure he sees everybody that people know to be associated with either of us."

"I'll take care of it. What airline and flight is he on?"

Carl laughed. "He's not on an airline. He's on a jet. Your tax dollars are hard at work transporting the Amazing Ray from Washington D.C. to Dallas, Texas."

"They've spent my money on less worthy causes. What are your tax dollars doing?"

"Mine are being used to provide a secure room guarded 24/7 by an elite squad of Secret Service Agents for two lovely ladies who will be very happy when April comes home."

I don't know if I was more shocked that the Federal Government was actually helping us out on this or that the most skeptical conspiracy theorist I've ever met was accepting the help. I found it ironic, but chose not to comment on it.

"Okay, we'll get Ray picked up. When are you coming back to Dallas?"

"Emily and Jade are staying in the Beltway. Courtney and I will meet up with y'all at the canyon when we can."

Only Carl can drive halfway across the country with three beautiful ladies and come back with one of the two who isn't his wife and still expect to stay happily married. I also chose not to mention that.

Instead, I finished going over the accommodations with Ramona and asked her if she could drop me off at Love Field. She agreed. On our way, I sent texts to everybody to let them know that Raymond needed to see everybody before they headed west. I couldn't tell anybody the reason, but nobody seemed to care about that. My army is as loyal as it is diverse and dangerous.

We got to the airport around five-twenty. Ramona offered to stay, but I had already kept her away too long from her new love, Sheldon. That left me with almost an hour to kill at the airport. But better to have time to kill than to interfere with budding love. Besides, time is just one of the things a detective sometimes has to kill in the line of duty.

Killing time at Love Field turned out to be much easier than I expected. Since the east terminal is mainly used for personal aircraft and small freight haulers, the only car rental options were about a mile away. By the time I rented a car using a name so fictitious I have to concentrate not to laugh every time I use it, it was almost six.

If anybody wondered why I rented a car, and then left it sitting while I walked back to the airport, they either weren't curious enough to ask or they never got the chance. It seldom bothers me that I'm one of the few people in the Lone Star State who doesn't drive, but at the moment it was a bit of an inconvenience.

As I sat in the terminal waiting for Raymond's plane to arrive, I mostly wondered if I deserved my army's loyalty and if we were dangerous enough to accomplish the mission. When the plane arrived, I heard it before I saw it. If I hadn't heard it first, I wouldn't have seen it until it was on the ground. I'm not an expert on planes, so I don't know what kind it was.

All I know is it was silver, loud and fast. I thought about asking Mistress Caroline if she could get us a couple. I didn't because I was afraid she might, and I had no idea what we'd do with them if we had them.

Amazing was carrying a metallic silver briefcase right out of a James Bond movie. The only thing missing was the handcuff to his wrist. I chose not to ask him about its contents, so as we walked to get the rental, he tried to amaze me with trivial facts about Palo Duro Canyon. No person on earth has seen him perform as often as I have, but I'll admit he again amazed me a little.

Once we were in the car on the way to Pegasus Investigations' office, he changed the subject. "I know you're way too cool to ask about the briefcase, but aren't you at least a little curious about why Carl insisted that y'all wait for me before leaving?"

I admitted to at least a slight curiosity. He positively beamed. "Dude, you are not going to believe what I learned to do. It makes every trick anybody in our show could do look like child's play. When we get to the office, you are going to be amazed."

I doubted it, but I didn't say so. When somebody called Amazing Ray tells you he is about to amaze you, there's nothing to be gained by disagreeing.

38   Covert Operatives

As we climbed the steps to the office, I briefly wondered if I should have called Jeff to let him know we were on our way. Guarding a fortress that doesn't need to be guarded can't be much fun. I hoped he hadn't developed an itchy trigger finger.

I needn't have worried. Jeff and Spineless Spicoli were playing Call of Duty on the X-Box system April had brought in shortly after she joined the agency. Sam The Man and Lamont were playing chess at the conference table. The only person who appeared even slightly interested in guarding the fortress was Jeff's former boss, Pat.

He sat on April's desk pointing a rifle at the door casually, as if he might want to shoot a rabbit if one happened to stand in front of him for a few minutes. The rifle was almost certainly older than me, and might have been older than Pat, but I had little doubt that it would still do what it was built to do. Old guys like Pat know that once you find a tool that works, there's no reason to replace it every time a new model comes on the market.

I decided on the grand entrance, "Ladies and Gentleman! The Amazing Raymond is in the house! He promises that he will dazzle us all with incredible feats. Gather Round! Gather Round!"

I shooed Pat off April's desk and Raymond to the chair behind it. Nobody looked like they expected to be amazed, but the chess board and the X-Box were abandoned as everybody assembled around the desk. I've seen Raymond perform hundreds of times, and he never once has looked comfortable as he begins. This was no exception.

"For the record, I never promised to dazzle anybody, let alone everybody. If I recall correctly, and I think we all know that I do, I only told Freak that he would be amazed."

Sam The Man and Spineless clapped. Show business people, and those who hang around show business people, learn how to show respect to performers. We all settled in and waited to be amazed by an Amazing Ray performance.

Raymond didn't actually give a performance. Instead he gave us a demonstration of technology that was nothing short of amazing. He altered our smart phones so that nobody could ever know we left

Dallas to go rescue April from the bastards who had taken her to a big hole in the ground near Amarillo, Texas.

Only Pat wasn't impressed, largely because he doesn't have a smart phone. Since he was well on his way to retiring by the time smart phones appeared on the scene, that made sense. He ran a detective agency in this town for decades, and has helped Pegasus Investigation many times.

As Raymond worked on the phones, Pat looked at me, "You gonna stay here tonight?"

"I guess so. Raymond's gonna be driving around being amazing with phones."

"Okay, I'm going home to sleep in my own bed. I'll come back in the morning to continue guarding this fortress."

"Sounds good, and thanks a lot."

"I'm happy to help. We've been through some wars together. Walk me to my car."

"Sure," I said. Pat's not a young man, but far too spry to need an escort to his car. I knew it was likely that he wanted to talk to me about something. I also knew I probably needed to hear whatever it was he wanted to tell me.

He didn't say anything as we walked to the parking lot across the street where he'd parked. I sensed that he was trying to decide how to say what he wanted to say. As he unlocked his Chevy Blazer, I touched his shoulder.

"What's on your mind, Pat? You can tell me. I can take it."

He sighed. "I suppose you can. I know you've got a lot on your mind with rescuing your wife and saving the office and all. I know you and Carl will work that out. I know how good you are."

He paused, I didn't hesitate, "It's not Carl and me, it's the whole army, you included. We're going to get her back because we're all good."

"Freak, I know you feel that way, but I know better. I'm an old man. My days as a hero are behind me. I understand that. I'm happy to hang around and guard a fortress that doesn't need guarding. I'm happy to bill you for my time. I'll be happy to cash the check you give me when this is all over. But, I have to tell you that you're making a big mistake."

"I'll bite. What big mistake am I making?"

"You're wasting Jeff's talents keeping him cooped up in your fortress."

"Am I? That fortress is the second most important thing in this battle. When we get April back, it is likely to be ground zero for the bad guys' next attack. Jeff's skills, and his reputation, are our first line of defense when that happens."

"I don't know if you really believe that, but I'll accept that you do. I'll put it a different way. "You're boring Jeff."

Pat pointed to Jeff's metallic silver Dodge Charger.

"Jeff did not replace his Mustang with Detroit's most fast and furious new muscle car, so he can park it on the street, while he sits in an office playing video games."

I knew that Jeff had replaced his Mustang because it never felt the same after he used it to tear all Hell out of a Saturn Sky, but Pat's point made sense.

"That's probably true," I told Pat. "I'll see what I can do."

I thought about Jeff as I climbed back to the office. As mad as he'd been when he tore up his Mustang, he had at least received some excitement and a story to tell.

I made a decision. It was an easy decision to make.

"Jeff, I'll stay here and guard the office tonight. You go home and pack. We're leaving for west Texas in the morning."

Jeff looked up excitedly, "Are we taking my car?"

"No, we're taking an RV." I noticed his excitement dwindling, so I continued, "I need you, not the car. We'll rent something acceptable when we get out there. That way if you have to ram into somebody again, you won't have to have ruined your baby."

His face brightened slightly, then dimmed. "Who's going to guard this place?"

"I'll have Pat find somebody. I need you on the front lines. You're not scared, are you?"

I knew he wasn't scared, and he knew I knew he wasn't scared. The only meaning fear has to guys like Jeff and me is a tool to be used to get other people to help us out.

He laughed, "You know I'm not. I'd just sort of accepted that this wasn't going be my time to shine."

"You always shine, Jeff. We both do. Go home and get packed, so we can go to BFE and rescue the one human being on the planet who shines brighter than either of us."

He readily agreed. As he left the office, I noticed he had some pep back in his step that I hadn't even noticed had been missing. As I wondered how long it had been missing, it occurred to me that Pegasus Investigations might need its Chief Morale Officer back almost as badly as I need my wife back. It almost as quickly occurred to me that nobody and nothing had ever needed anything almost as badly as I needed April back.

39   Bad People

In the morning around eleven, Larry Joe picked Jeff and me up at the office. Pat and three large associates had been with us for a couple of hours showing each other their guns and trading tall tales. At one point, I got bored, and asked Pat if he was paying for the help or if I was paying for it.

The largest of the three men answered, "We all signed on as volunteers. We're going to be famous bodyguards one day, and having the legendary April Rose, Freak Show and Pegasus Investigations as references is going to get that started."

He blushed just a little before he continued, "If that's all right, I mean. I just sort of assumed it would be okay?"

I assured him it would be fine, and they all went back to comparing weapons and lying to each other. I thought about bringing Excalibur into the discussion, but I was afraid it might break their confidence.

It only took a few minutes to get to Fuel City from the office. Larry Joe parked his Ford F350 beside an impressive looking RV. Jeff went inside to get some of the tacos that make Fuel City one of the very few gas stations in the world actually famous for its food.

Larry Joe went to talk to the man who'd delivered the RV, while I took a look at the RV's exterior. I expected to have plenty of time to look at the interior on the way to Palo Duro Canyon.

"Well, Pardner, whaddya think of this contraption?"

"Arkansas plates, huh? Nice touch. You think of everything."

"I reckon thar ain't no call here for suckin' up, Sonny Boy"

"I'm not sucking up; I'm just stating fact."

"I reckon ah'll just let that be. You're sure Jeff can drive this thang. It's a dam sight bigger'n any thang Ah've ever seen him up on."

I laughed out loud. "Okay, maybe you don't think of everything. You apparently didn't think to investigate Jeff's background when I told you Pegasus was hiring him. If it has wheels and a motor, Jeff can drive it."

I didn't bother to mention that if it didn't have wheels or a motor, Jeff could build the motor, make and install some wheels and find a way to turn it into a working automobile pretty much no matter what it had been originally built to be.

Jeff came out of Fuel City with three bags of tacos.

As he handed one to Larry Joe, I asked him, "Did you notice the Arkansas plates?"

"I did, but I was far more impressed by the Ellsworth Truth SST.2 XTR mountain bikes." He looked at Larry Joe. "How'd we get hooked up with these bad boys?"

Larry Joe shrugged, "I reckoned y'all might have a hankerin' for bikes, so I called up a pardner and let him know about the posse. He set us up with eight of these. How much am I gonna be out if Sonny Boy forgets to bring 'em back."

Jeff looked over the bikes more carefully before answering. "I'd say somewhere between sixty thousand and ninety thousand. These two aren't tricked out the same way so it could vary. Base price is about seven thousand."

Larry Joe sighed, then looked at me, "Sonny Boy, I reckon you should make sure Ah get at least one of them bikes back so Ah can pay for your funeral."

I promised I would get at least one back to him, and Jeff and I got in the RV. I sat in the passenger seat, and finally opened Raymond's metal case with no idea what to expect. If I'd taken the time to try to guess, it would have been time wasted.

I whistled when I picked up the first file folder. I don't know how many civilians ever get their hands on a copy of a real top-secret government file, but I suspect it's a pretty exclusive group. Ray had accompanied The Great Detective to Washington D.C. in the hopes that he might at least get a glimpse of some and we'd have an Amazing Ray version of a copy of a few.

Instead, we had not a few, but a briefcase full of them. Not only that, they came from different branches of the government. Of the first seven I saw, which turned out to be the ones that interested me the most, three were from the Central Intelligence Agency and four were from the Federal Bureau of Investigations.

Carl has told me very little about his relationship with Courtney Winchester or what she does for a living. I know she works for the government and that the lady has helped us out on a handful of cases, but that's about it. Apparently, there is much more to be known about both subjects.

I put that thought aside and dug into the files. The first two contained different versions of the same information regarding Sal Perlini. According to both versions, he is suspected of being involved in everything from 9/11 to the Boston Marathon bombing, but not one shred of actionable evidence has ever been found to connect him to anything more serious than a bar fight.

Even his connection to the bar fight seems tenuous, at best. The patron whose brawling skills failed him in the fight, turned out to have a pistol which he never brandished that had once belonged to Sal Perlini. My biggest takeaway from that incident is that the National Rifle Association might have a point about how much the government wants to know about gun ownership.

The other five files concerned people who had been more concretely connected to criminal activity, a whole bunch of criminal activity. The first three of the five were on the FBI's most wanted list in the category: wanted dead or alive. I had not previously been sure that 'Wanted: Dead or Alive' existed as anything other than a plot device for Hollywood westerns.

I also hadn't realized that reward money offered could be in the millions. The only rewards I currently sought were April's million dollar smile and her safety, but I filed that information away for safekeeping as I began to peruse the CIA files on two Chechen Nationals whose acts of terrorism have led to them being tried in absentia and convicted by the United States, two other countries allied with the United States, and one country most definitely not allied with the United States.

The one thing all five of them had in common is that each had been spotted by the agents who were assigned to keep April from being kidnapped in the hours leading up to her kidnapping. This last crime of theirs was the one that concerned me the most. Actually, it was the only one that concerned me.

I needed to get April away from these bastards sooner, rather than later. I also needed to do it without giving them access to the secret staircase that led from our office to the various tunnels under downtown Dallas, and who knows where else. I don't believe all, or even most, of Carl's conspiracy theories, but I believe him when he says that nobody alive knows exactly where all of those tunnels go.

I was trying to decide whether to dive into the rest of the files first or reheat the remaining Fuel City tacos when my phone rang. Without even looking at my phone, I sensed that this would be the call Carl and I knew would eventually come. I told Jeff to pull over to the shoulder of US 287 and kill the engine. I strolled to the back of the RV and answered as soon as I heard the motor cut off.

40   Good Questions

I answered in my most professional voice, "Pegasus Investigations, Dallas Premiere Detective Agency."

"Indeed? I had been warned to expect confidence from the arrogant young Freak Show. That information appears to be correct. I intend to break you of that confidence."

"Others have tried. Who is this?"

"You do not need to know who I am. You only need to know who I have taken. I know you already know who I have taken. She's a very pretty and delightful young lady. You must miss her terribly by now. I would think you would be eager now to discuss my price."

The voice was cold and hard. The accent was Northeastern United States. I presumed he was one of the three Americans who had taken my wife. From the files, I'd learned that two of the American kidnappers, Jimmy Ray Poteet and Jerome Thibodeaux, were from Oklahoma and Louisiana, respectively, so I presumed I was talking to Cliff Parsons of Stamford, Connecticut.

Some societies believe there is power to be had in knowing your adversary's name. Amazing Ray liked to use the phrase, 'I have the advantage of you' in his performances when he would taunt a D-List celebrity who had come to a show not expecting to be singled out.

I've never believed in that particular brand of hocus-pocus, but I had noticed that sometimes his foils would squirm uncomfortably. I kept that idea in reserve, but chose to not act on it immediately. Instead, I chose to do what April often says that I do best. I fronted.

"Thank you for calling, but I see no reason to discuss price at this time."

I hoped it would shake him up a little, and it did. It actually shook him up enough that he hung up the phone. I knew he would call back soon, and I decided to take the offensive when he did. When my phone rang again, I answered immediately.

"Mr. Parsons, I presume? I admire your tenacity as a salesman, but as I told you a minute ago, I'm not interested in discussing price at this time."

For a man who thought he held the high card, he didn't sound very confident, "How do you know my name?"

"I know the name of many people, Cliff. Don't be alarmed. It's not the policy of the United States Government or Pegasus Investigations to negotiate with terrorists. However, if you'll let me talk to your hostage, I might be willing to make an exception."

"I can't do that. She's not here."

"Where is she, Cliff?"

"Stop calling me that!"

I had no idea why he didn't want to be called by his name, but I started to believe the legends about the power of knowing an adversary's name.

"Will do, Mr. Parsons," I lied. "Where is your hostage?"

"You don't need to know that, Mr Scholes."

"I do if I'm going to talk to you about this."

"Perhaps I should look for another buyer. In many parts of the world, blonde women fetch a high price. Your wife is in extremely mint condition. I expect I could fetch a pretty penny for her."

"Can any of those customers offer you the price you are hoping to extract from me?"

"Perhaps not, but the price will be high. I might like an offer well enough to take it if you won't even negotiate. If I do, where will that leave you, Mr. Show?"

I said a prayer to The God I'd only recently begun to believe in and hoped April was right about my ability to front.

"I suppose, it would leave me one blonde short. The funny thing is that this bustling, vibrant city is absolutely teeming with blondes, beautiful blondes at that. Unlike, you sir, I've never found myself having to resort to kidnapping to acquire one."

"Indeed? I'd been led to believe that this one was special to you. If not, I suppose I could just dispose of her and kidnap somebody else."

"They're all special to me, Cliff. If you dispose of her in a manner not to my liking, you won't get a chance to pick another. Like most collectors, I value what I collect."

"I see I have not yet broken your confidence. Trust me, I will."

Finally the conversation took a turn so that I no longer needed to front.

"Two things will never happen! I will never trust you, and you will never break my confidence."

"Perhaps I should call your partner; he might understand better that you are completely outgunned here."

I thought about the army Mistress Caroline and I had assembled and how few details about said army I had shared with Carl. I didn't laugh out loud, but I smiled. "I'd love to hear it. Why don't you come over to my house and make the call on my speaker phone? You do know where I live, right?"

He hung up without answering, but in doing so, he answered the most important question I had. If he knew I was hours away from Dallas, he'd have called my bluff. Wherever Amazing Raymond had learned to doctor our phones, he'd learned it well.

Cliff Parson and his evil minions thought I was pacing the floor of my beautiful house in Dallas. They had no idea that I and the knights of my army were on the way to Palo Duro Canyon to slay the dragons and rescue the princess, not necessarily in that order.

As we turned onto I-40, my phone rang. I didn't recognize the number, so I answered, "Pegasus Investigations."

"Where are you? I thought you'd be here by now." Rachel sounded excited in a good way, like a school girl with a good report card to hand her parents.

"We were unavoidably detained. We should be there in about an hour."

"Okay. Don't be detained again. We have news. Caroline wants to tell you herself, but I'm busting at the seams. If you don't get here quick, I'm going to have to tell you myself."

I figured out a long time ago that Mistress Caroline is more protective of her girls than she is a danger to them. Even so, I saw no reason to risk getting her mad at Rachel, or me, for that matter.

"I trust this is news that I'm going to like?"

"I told you, Caroline wants to tell you. Hurry, we'll be waiting at the RV park."

An hour later, Mistress Caroline climbed onboard. Rachel and Sam The Man followed closely at her heels. Even on the carpeted floor of the RV, her heels announced her presence and her expectation that the room would be hers to command.

She put a business card on the table as the five of us sat in the cozy living area. The calling card identified her as Caroline Throckmorton, Chapter President of Greater Atlanta Ladies Bird Watching Society. It also listed an address in Buckhead, Georgia and a phone number. I saw no reason to ask if the number and address would stand scrutiny.

I smiled at Caroline, who smiled back. "The ladies and I are looking for a strikingly beautiful rare bird."

"Have you found her?"

"No actual sighting yet, but I think we know where she is. The ladies of the club are rotating around the area. If she appears even for a second, we'll know. Even if she doesn't, we will have pictures of anybody who might have seen her."

"That was quick. How sure are we?"

"That is a complicated question. Autumn Quake Hearer is convinced. She could be wrong, but I believe her. I asked her to meet us here, but she declined. She says she must comfort the canyon until the torture ends."

I didn't even pretend not to be skeptical of the old woman. "Excuse me? She seriously thinks somebody is torturing a canyon?"

Mistress Caroline frowned. "I misspoke. Autumn did not use the word 'torture.' What Autumn said is that somebody created a cave in a part of the canyon that the Spirits did not intend to have a cave. She also said the new cave is being bombarded with a steady stream of insanely loud music."

The light dawned on me, "Music torture. That's the type of thing these bastards would use. Let's go get her."

"It's not that easy. The cave is far underground. My ladies have found the entrance, but we can't just march in there. The actual hide out is behind two other caves. If we hadn't seen men going in and out, we never would have found it. It is safe to presume that the entrance is secured, either by force or by a trap of some type. That grotto here in West Texas is most likely as impenetrable as the caves in Afghanistan."

I sighed. We could probably penetrate it, eventually, but where would that leave April? I glanced at Rachel.

"Are we sure this is good news?"

Mistress Caroline answered for her. "Good question, but I think it is. For one thing, knowing where she is the first step to getting her back. For another, music torture is no walk in the park, but it leaves no permanent damage. These aren't boy scouts we're dealing with. Did you expect them to be baking her cookies and singing camp fire songs while they held her?"

She had a valid point. A point I'd been trying to repress in an attempt to maintain my sanity. It was almost certainly time to stop worrying about my sanity and start worrying about April's.

41   Paha Kaga

"I trust you have a good reason that I needed to be here. Even during the silence, I should be with my land."

Autumn agreed to leave her land to meet with my team only during the dawn hour, because she said the canyon was most at peace at that time of day. After four days at Palo Duro Canyon, including three days with The Great Detective and the mysterious Courtney Remington with us, we'd accomplished a few things, but not enough.

The bird watchers had confirmed that Sal Perlini had not visited the cave, but that the other five suspects had been there at various times, and in various quantities; never less than two. No other visitors had been seen.

Carl answered her question for me. "We do have a good reason, Madam. I promise."

That satisfied her. "Okay, I will help if I can."

"You can." I assured her. "Lamont, please tell her what you told me last night."

Lamont cleared his throat, "The men who dug those caves into your land almost certainly built them as copies of the ones our Military, and the Soviet Military before it, found to be difficult to breach in Afghanistan."

"Of course, I knew this was the work of the U.S. Government. I grow weary of the lies…"

Courtney spoke firmly, "Not that it matters, but these men are not affiliated with the Government. They are rogues."

"You sound like you believe that. I do not. The liars in your Government have forked tongues and cannot be trusted."

Courtney smiled sadly. "Ms. Quake Hearer, as it applies to this situation, I am the United States Government. I assure you these men are not with us. I know they've been terminated, because I'm the person who fired their sorry asses."

Even Carl looked shocked by that revelation. This might have been a good time for the infamous Pegasus Investigations silent routine, but I didn't have time for that. April was a few miles away in an underground prison.

"Lamont, please continue," I said.

"Uh, okay, the thing is, I've been in those caves. It's not enough to have a bunker that's hard to penetrate. You have to have a way to get out the other side if someone does penetrate it. There should be a way out other than the entrance we've been watching."

Mistress Caroline nodded. I got the feeling she wondered why she hadn't thought of that, but she said nothing.

Autumn Quake Hearer looked puzzled. "How does that justify me being here?"

I answered quickly, "We hope you can find the back door. Perhaps some disturbance to the land occurred as they were creating it."

She laughed, "I do not need to find it. It was found many moons ago; even before my people arrived here. It is the only part of their labyrinth that was here when the Kiowa and the Comanche arrived on this land. It is the Paha Kaga."

I didn't like the way she said the phrase, but I had to ask. "What's that in English?"

"There is no literal translation, but you can think of it as the devils stair case."

"I see, take us to it and let's get April back."

"I can not do that." The old woman was not laughing now. "My people do not go where the Spirits tell us not to go."

"Maybe you better tell us about this stair case. I respect that you will not go there. I even respect your reason. I probably shouldn't go there, either. As you know, however, I have no choice."

Autumn reached her hand out to me, and I took it. Where only days ago she had shook my hand firmly and quickly in a manner which belied her age, today her hand felt like that of an old lady. It felt cold and weak, and it trembled. She made no move to withdraw it, so I held it in what I hoped was a firm, yet tender way.

"I suppose you must at that. I could tell you in many ways how much safer it would be to shoot your way in through whatever defenses these men have put in place at the cave entrance you would not believe me."

I looked into her eyes and saw that her hand was shaking in fear for me, not for herself. If I truly believed in her powers, and I saw no reason not to believe, maybe I would be wise to listen. Shooting our way into that cave didn't sound like a great plan, but we definitely had the arsenal for it.

"Tell me about this Paha Kaga. If I'm going to dance with the devil, I should at least know the tune."

She pulled back her hand. "You would mock me?"

I reached for her hand, and when she reached to slap me away with her other hand, I grasped them both and cupped them in my own.

"I would never mock you. I'm not promising that you can talk me out of going there, but I should be armed with as much information as possible before I do. You are my only source of that information. Please tell me about it."

She smiled. "Now, I see. You do not mock me. You mock death, and the devils that accompany it. Many great Kiowa and Comanche warriors had that spirit. Both tribes would have been proud to have you as a member, or as a Chief. I noticed with interest that for days, your troops have surveyed the battlefield while you sat in an air cooled trailer."

She paused. If she was waiting for me to justify that, she was going to be disappointed. Apparently, she wasn't.

"I do not deny that I doubted if you were fit to be Chief. Just now, my doubts proved unfounded. When I warned you about Paha Kaga, you did not say you had to send your troops there, you said you had to go."

"Perhaps your doubts are not unfounded. My troops and I are as one to me. When we know what needs to be done, we will know which of us will go. If a sharp shooter is needed, Lamont will go."

I looked at Lamont, and he nodded. "I've already faced the Devil twice and I'm still here. I'll be glad to do it again, if it might get April back."

I continued, "If we need to push a boulder down the staircase, Sam The Man will go."

"I may go anyway, Boss. I've always wanted to meet that devil fellow."

Autumn's grip on my hands tightened. She was no longer shaking. "I get it. I misjudged you. I said I would not do that again, but I did. Need I apologize?"

She took her hands out of mine, but maintained eye contact with a steady hazel eyed stare that seemed to reach past my eyes and deep into my soul.

"No ma'am, you do not. But I do wish you'd tell me about the stairs my entire army is about to face. How many Native American skeletons are we going to have to step over to get to the bottom?"

"You will not find our bones there. We have avoided those stairs far longer than the bones of the lost stay in this world. When the Kiowa first came to the area, the Comanche warned us to stay away from those steps. The truce between our tribes was young then, so the Kiowa wondered if there was treasure to be had. We decided to look."

"Was there?" I asked.

"Nobody knows. The seers went first. What they saw is what they named it."

"They saw the devil?"

"No, my young warrior friend, they did not see the devil. They saw hordes of devils. You should not think of it as the stair case of the devil; it is the stair case of many devils."

"Then we will fight hordes of devils. Did they pass down descriptions of these devils?"

"But, of course. My people pass everything down. They saw creatures with many eyes and many legs feasting greedily on the flesh of men. They saw men who could walk on ceilings disappearing into the very air around them. They saw fire raining down from the sky…"

She continued naming off devils, but I lost interest long before she finished. I love a good fortune teller as much as the next guy, but once I know what my future holds, I prefer to act on it.

42   Insane Plans

"Seriously, Freak? That's your plan! You want me to walk down the devils stair case with my babies and rescue April. I know I volunteered us for this, but I thought you might find some sane way we could help."

"What's not sane about this plan?"

"For goodness sake, Freak. I'm Catholic; I can't just forsake my religion to walk with the Devil."

I briefly wondered how a Comanche or Kiowa chief would handle a reluctant warrior who happened to be a Catholic lesbian and was in a bad mood because she left her girlfriend at home seven hours away.

I carefully omitted my theory that some of the devils the stairs took their name from are her little lovelies.

Instead, I said, "Autumn said it is not a literal translation. This stair case probably doesn't belong to the same devil the pope keeps tweeting about."

"Thanks. Even without that, I'm ready. When do we go?"

"We need to be ready to go at any moment. The next time there are only two thugs in the grotto, we...."

"Uh, Freak, there's one little problem."

"What's the problem?"

"Miss Lickety Split is not an automatic repeating weapon. Her poison won't be lethal after the first bite."

Mistress Caroline smiled as she answered, "She won't have to kill them both. The Greater Atlanta Ladies Bird Watching Society will take care of the other one."

"How are you going to do that?"

She smiled again; she was most definitely smiling too often for my taste these days. She answered, "With the eternal knowledge of the ages, the unequaled wisdom of age, the enchanting beauty of youth and an extremely powerful tranquilizer."

Bobbie Jo didn't look impressed.

"If you need more detail, we're going to make a little noise at the entrance to the cave. When one of them comes to investigate, we'll say we saw a flame colored tanager enter this cave, and we absolutely must get a picture of it. At least that's the explanation we'll be giving until the tranquilizer darts Jeff and Lamont are going to shoot him with take affect."

"What if he doesn't ask for an explanation? What if he just starts shooting people?"

"He won't, but if he does, he'll have to try to drag the bodies back into the cave. The boys will still shoot him with the darts. We'll just have to bury a good soldier or two."

Bobbie Jo showed us the resolute look that she always has when she doesn't want to appear nervous even though she's scared to death. The first time I saw that look was when she came out to her parents. It's been a long, long time since I've seen it. The Kiowa and Comanche Chief probably knew what to do at a time like this.

I didn't, but it turned out I didn't need to know. Spineless Spicoli and the Amazing Ray chose this most opportune moment to enter the RV that currently served as headquarters.

They didn't say anything immediately, so I prompted, "Well?"

Spicoli answered, "Just like the old lady described it: a spiral stair case made of packed mud. At the bottom, it opens into another room. The staircase is narrow enough that I was able to crab-crawl at ceiling level. "April, or a blonde who looks like her from behind is perched on a wood veneer table with her arms tied behind her.

He paused to take a breath. "She's sitting like a catcher would sit if catchers wore skimpy outfits and high-heeled pumps instead of body armor and cleats. She's also wearing earbuds, and the music is so loud it was disturbing even from the stairs we were observing from."

I didn't ask Spicoli if he'd been seen. He would have mentioned if he had. Besides, if he'd been seen he probably would be dead now. I didn't like where that thought led my thoughts, so I asked Raymond, "Any other details we need to know, Amazing?"

Raymond said, "Sixty–seven total steps, the first twenty are steep and head west..."

I interrupted, "Just the ones we need to know, Raymond. When this is over, I'll book us in Vegas again and you can tell it all."

"I think this could matter. What light there is, and it is enough, comes down through various tiny holes, like tiny skylights. On a moonless night or if the sun is in the wrong place, it might be too dark to see."

"Okay, go on."

Raymond gave us the details without his usual showmanship. When he'd finished, I addressed the team.

"All set then, we get all the troops to the rim of the canyon."

I looked at BJ, "Including yours, my dear. We don't want to be waiting for Miss Lickety Split when the game is afoot.

Bobbie Jo nodded. I looked around the room. "Okay then, everybody knows the plan and their role in it. Anybody have any questions?"

Bobbie Jo had one. "What does Carl think about this plan?"

"If I ever tell him about it, I'll let you know."

Seven hours later, I was standing in Paha Kaga with a pair of wire clippers in my hand. If my count was correct, I was sixteen steps above a manmade cave where I had every reason to believe a handful of bastards were torturing my wife. Bobbie Jo was one stair step behind me with one tarantula on each shoulder and the eight-eyed devil of Kiowa Indian prophecy in a cute little purple box that she bought at a thrift store in Cleburne.

Even from here we could hear the music from below. I'm not sure why the military decided a great way to get secrets from suspects is to blast them with loud music. In Deep Ellum, it's the alcohol, not the music that makes people talk.

I looked at my watch. It was 5:58. Mistress Caroline had guaranteed that her team would distract one of the bad guys at 6:05. I showed the watch to Bobbie Jo. I knew she didn't need to see it; I just needed something to do to pass the time. At 6:03, she opened the purple box and picked up the eight limbed, eight eyed devil she called Miss Lickety Split.

Even though Bobbie Jo was wearing a thick leather work glove, this was the first moment where something might go terribly wrong. If the spider bit the glove, it wouldn't hurt Bobbie Jo, but it would disarm the arachnid soldier we were counting on. I looked the question to her.

With her ungloved hand, she gave me one thumb up. We started down the stairs. At the last step we saw the scene. April was trussed up exactly as Spicoli had described. Jimmy Ray Poteet was standing in front of her randomly waving around a gun that looked like April's as he watched her listen to music so loud that even though it was through ear buds, I heard it clearly enough to recognize it as Long Sword Spectacular's 'Revelation.'

I saw Bobbie Jo's laser light land on the thug's ankle only seconds before Miss Lickety Split did what she was here to do. As soon as Jimmy Ray hit the ground, I ran to April and snipped the earphone cable. The music stopped immediately. As I untied April, I glanced at Bobbie Jo. Instead of gathering up her spiders, she was checking for a pulse with her free hand and picking up the gun with her other.

For a second, I thought I heard Rachel scream in the distance, but it didn't last long enough for me to be sure. The next thing I heard was much clearer.

"Jimmy Ray, why did you turn off the music?"

Since Jimmy Ray wasn't going to be answering, April decided maybe she should. "Because he figured out it's not going to work. If I had anything to say, I'd have already said it."

Bobbie Jo now had the laser pointer in one hand and was walking toward the voice. Ten feet in front of her, Miss Lickety Split was following the green dot more faithfully than Pavlov's dogs ever answered a bell.

When Jerome Thibodeaux rounded the corner, he saw the green dot and the spider at the same time. "What the Hell is that?"

He didn't wait for an answer. Instead, he tried to empty the magazine of his semiautomatic pistol into the sandy floor of Palo Duro Canyon. He failed because Bobbie Jo shot him once in the head and once in the heart with Jerome's pistol.

Two thugs were dead. April was loose, but I had a real bad feeling that the price had been high. I could only think of one reason why Mistress Caroline's bird watchers hadn't followed Jerome into the cave. It was a reason that would also explain why I heard Rachel scream.

"Bobbie Jo, can you go check on the others?" I tried to sound calm as I said it, but I'm sure I failed.

She started walking without saying a word or lowering her gun. She probably shared my pessimism. I noticed that only two spiders accompanied her.

I held April in my arms, "Are you okay, darling?"

"No, but I will be."

"Was it bad?"

"Yes, but I've seen worse."

"Can I help?"

"You already have."

"Do you want to talk about it?"

She did not want to talk about it. She just wanted to be held, so I held her. I held her for a long time.

43   Plausible Deniabilities

"Well, needless to say, that didn't go according to plan." Mistress Caroline had apparently mastered the art of the understatement. "He never got close enough for Jeff or Lamont to shoot, and the second we started the explanation. He reached into his pocket. I thought he was reaching for his gun."

She paused. Her cavalier attitude about burying soldiers and moving on clearly was a façade. Whatever faults Mistress Caroline may have, not caring about her people isn't one of them.

I prompted her, "But he wasn't?"

"No, thank the goddesses! He must have had some kind of remote in his pocket. A wall simply fell out of ceiling and blocked the entrance to the second cave. We were left staring at a wall of adobe bricks with a sign stating that this was private property, not park land."

Carl said, "Which is, in fact, completely true. That cave is at least a mile from the actual park."

Mistress Caroline nodded, "We knew that going in. We just didn't expect them to let us know in that particular manner.

Bobbie Jo said, "Well that explains why we had to leave the way we came in. What do we do now?"

Carl answered that one. "I think we wait until Courtney gets back from the cave. This may be a good time to turn this over to her team."

I doubted that a little, and I could tell from the look on Mistress Caroline's face that she had already completely dismissed the idea.

Bobbie Jo said, "I think this would be a good time to bury our fallen soldier."

"Fallen soldier? Who died?"

"Carl, my friend, you do not want to know."

Carl looked from me to Bobbie Jo and back. "You're right. I'm going back to my cabin. Make sure the fallen soldier gets a proper sendoff."

We buried Miss Lickety Split in land that Autumn Quake Hearer assured us was a sacred spot for fallen heroes. She even

Brian D. Eyre

admitted that sometimes the seers' visions could be misinterpreted. She still won't go near Paha Kaga, though. After the funeral, we went back to the cabin which now served as headquarters to hear what Courtney had to say.

She got right to the point. "The US Government has no official interest in anything that has happened in that cave thus far. The fake door is still blocking the cave entrance. The next people to enter that cave will find two men who appear to have shot each other and an empty table with a pile of ropes scattered around it."

I asked, "Any idea how soon somebody is likely to enter that cave?"

She smiled, "I have a pretty good idea; Cliff Parsons and two Chechen Nationals whose names I cannot pronounce, were sighted leaving Dallas in a white Econoline van about two hours ago. At their current rate, they should be here around seven-thirty."

Carl immediately asked the right question. "How are they likely to react to the missing hostage?"

Courtney smiled. It was a smile that would not have been out of character for Mistress Caroline. "It might be better for all of us if they don't get much chance to react to that situation."

Mistress Caroline smiled in kind. "In that case it might be better if they didn't arrive until after nine."

Courtney nodded and smiled again. "Of course, that would be much better. I believe West Bound 287 is long overdue for a drug trafficking crackdown. My work here is done. I'm going to go arrange the checkpoints. If you're expecting any company from the east, expect two hour delays. Carl, would you be kind enough to walk me to my car?"

Of course, he would be kind enough. When they were gone, Mistress Caroline looked at me. "Did the United States Government just give us permission to kill three people?"

"Not really," I answered. "Permission to kill these three was granted when the bastards made the FBI's 'wanted dead or alive' list. All she did was promise to arrange for them to arrive after dark, to make it easier for us to ambush them."

"I don't plan to ambush anybody."

200

Since I didn't actually have a plan, I asked her to share hers. As she did, I realized that even if I'd had a plan, it wouldn't have been as good as hers. Mistress Caroline was going to avenge April's kidnapping, eliminate three more mercenaries who pose a threat to the security of our country, and make an old Indian woman very happy.

All I had to do was convince everybody associated with Pegasus Investigation to get as far away from Palo Duro Canyon as we could get before sundown and make sure we locked down unimpeachable alibis in the process. Granted, my part in the plan was much harder than her part, but I didn't mind. I'm always up for a challenge.

It took some convincing. April actually had to beg Sam The Man and Rachel to come with us, but by six o'clock, almost every member of our army that could be connected to Pegasus Investigations was on the highway out of the Canyon. Only Mistress Caroline and the Greater Atlanta Women's Bird Watching Society were left in Palo Duro Canyon.

By nine-thirty, the rest of our army was at the Parkway Grill in Wichita Falls watching the Rangers play the Angels. Even though only a couple of us were big fans, we cheered loudly enough to be sure everybody in the bar could provide an alibi.

Even without that, the waitress would certainly remember us since the group, especially Spicoli and Raymond, had her bringing us pitchers of beer almost as fast as the bartender could pour them. Only Lamont, Osalumense and I abstained, although I noticed that Carl was nursing his beer.

A little after ten, Rachel looked down at her phone. She texted back and forth for a couple minutes, then looked up.

"It's over."

Carl asked immediately, "Any problems?"

"Nope. It went exactly as planned.

As she talked, a scroll went across the bottom of the televisions, 'Explosion in Canyon, Texas: at least twenty dead, hundreds missing.'

April squeezed my hand and shrieked, "Twenty?"

Carl gently put his hand on her other hand. "It's okay, by tomorrow, it will be down to ten. When they finish the investigation, it will be down to five."

Amazing Raymond took a drink and added, "He's right. It always works that way. The press always exaggerates the body count in the immediate aftermath of a tragedy. For example, 2977 people died in the attacks on 9/11. At the time, at least three news outlets (and I use that term loosely) reported that over 25,000 had been killed. I have other examples, if it will help."

April shook her head, and Raymond left it at that.

Carl continued, "The important thing is that it worked. We've won the battle."

Rachel asked, "Only the battle, not the war?"

Carl, of course, didn't answer immediately. When he finally did answer, he didn't do much to relax the assembled army. I'm guessing that's the way he intended it.

"Battle or war; word choice isn't important. Even if we won the war, it doesn't keep a new war from starting at any time."

Raymond quickly downed his beer and slammed the mug on the table. "Do we have to sit back and wait for somebody to start it again, or can we take the fight to them?"

Sam The Man stood up and high-fived Raymond in what may have been the most poorly executed high-five in the history of ever. Raymond's beer consumption may have factored into that situation, but I think it was mostly a height differential issue.

"I like the way you think, my man!" He turned to me "We're all fired up, My Lord. Can't we take the fight to the enemy instead of waiting on them to bring the fight to us?"

I deferred to The Great Detective who was busy topping off his beer mug from one of the pitchers of beer. Only after he'd finished pouring, did he answer.

"I believe we should let Ms. Remington's department have the next move. They may not be any better at killing terrorists than we are, but I guarantee you they are better at hiding the bodies."

He had a valid point. Everybody acknowledged that for now we should stand down, sit tight and stay ready. When that was settled, I looked at Spicoli.

"Are you in for round two if it comes to it?"

He smiled. "I wouldn't miss it for the world, Freak!"

"Good. Make sure I know how to reach you before you leave town again."

Rachel giggled. Spicoli's smile widened.

"I take it you didn't hear. I'm going to be around for the foreseeable future. I accepted a job offer from Mistress Caroline."

I don't shock easily, and when I am shocked, I usually hide it pretty well. This time I didn't hide my surprise at all.

"What are you going to be doing for her, Spicoli?"

Rachel hadn't stopped giggling. Now she was laughing uncontrollably. Spicoli barely managed not to laugh as he replied.

"I'm afraid I'm not at liberty to discuss the nature of the position. If I told you, Rachel would have to kill both of us."

Now our entire party was laughing, myself included. Eventually we got back to watching the game and the periodic interruptions of the game to update the tragic events in Pala Duro Canyon.

Just before midnight, the Rangers rallied to take a lead over the Angels, and the waitress announced last call. We ordered a couple more pitchers and hung around to watch Tanner Scheppers nail down his second major league save.

By one in the morning our travelling party was on the way back to Dallas. By three, April and I were in bed trying without success to fall asleep. We spent the next two days watching news coverage of the terrible tragedy in Palo Duro Canyon.

As Carl had predicted, the news reports fluctuated about how many had died. Several locals were interviewed who swore they'd seen strange lights in the sky just before the explosion.

Others swore it had just blown up with no warning. The opinions of the television experts tended to vary by network and time of day. Thursday night, I fell asleep on the couch with April in my arms and the television still spouting theories in the background. I slept fitfully as I dreamed about spiders and fires and remote controls.

The dreams that I found most disturbing were the ones that involved remote controls.

44   Castle Doctrine

Friday morning, my phone woke me up around eight o'clock. I normally hate that, but I didn't mind this call.

"Good morning, Boss. How's the nation's capital treating you?"

He laughed, "Better than it usually does. I'm with Emily and Jade at Dulles Airport waiting to board. This afternoon, the investigation into the explosion in Palo Duro Canyon will conclude with a press conference."

He paused, so I humored him. "Will the spokesman mention any names that we know?

"It will, indeed. Three Americans and two Chechen Nationals will be mentioned by name as incompetent terrorists who foolishly set off a bomb in their own lair. No civilians were killed or injured."

We both knew that's not what happened. I didn't much mind that the Government was covering up our role in the affair, but I knew Carl was going to use this episode to defend every conspiracy theory he fixates on for the rest of forever. All good things come with a cost.

When I hung up the phone, April asked, "Well?"

"As Carl predicted the final death toll has been announced at five. This afternoon at a press conference, the Feds will announce that five idiots accidently blew up their own cave."

"In a way, that's what happened."

I asked, "How so?"

"There are probably a hundred and fifty million women in this country they could have kidnapped and lived to tell about it. But they accidently kidnapped the wife of The Absolutely Incredible Freak Show. Some terrorist bastards just can't buy a break."

I saw no reason to mention that they didn't accidently choose her to kidnap. I was too happy seeing a glimmer of the joie d'vivre that made April famous to risk mentioning that little detail.

We ate breakfast in reasonably comfortable silence. After we finished the dishes, April showed some of the resilience that isn't what makes her famous, but probably should be.

"I'm coming to the office this morning. You can't stop me."

I knew I couldn't stop her, nor did I want to stop her. After her ordeal, I couldn't blame her for wanting to get back to work.

"You want to drive, or should we just walk?" I asked.

She picked up her car keys off the counter in answer, and I followed her out the front door toward her car. At the curb, she paused and put the keys in her purse.

"We'll walk. I have to learn to walk again. I can't live my life in fear again. That's not living."

I held out my hand, and she took it. "You can't live forever in fear, but if you're still nervous now, it's understandable. You've been through Hell. It's okay to come back slowly."

"Not for me, it isn't. Let's go to work."

That's why April was sitting at her normal desk working on the PC, and I was at the conference table pretending not to watch her when Sal Perlini climbed the stairs into the waiting room. He didn't ring the bell. He simply sat down.

As the man who built this fortress, Perlini knew better than anybody that the bell was there so potential clients wouldn't know we could see their every move from inside. He also knew the only way he could enter is if we opened the door to admit him. He took a seat and seemed ready to wait as long as it took.

April looked at me. "You should let him in."

"Why?"

"He might be a client."

"He might also be a threat."

"We're detectives, Darling. That's always been true of everybody who climbs those stairs, and it always will be true. Unless you're ready to retire, let him in."

As always, April made a valid point. I walked into my office and picked up the Colt .45 that Mistress Caroline had given me and walked to the door which separates the waiting room from the office. With Excalibur at my side, I nodded for April to unlock the door. When she did, I opened the door. I hoped the gun would be the first thing Sal noticed. It worked.

"Damn, Freak. That's some serious hardware. Don't shoot."

"I won't." I assured him, "Unless you give me a reason."

"Freak, I'm not even packing heat. I just came by to talk. Can I come in?"

I nodded and pointed him toward the conference table. He walked that way, but hesitated before sitting. "Frisk me, if you want."

I did want, and I did frisk him. April pointed my gun at him while I did so. When I was sure he was clean, April handed me my gun and went back to her desk. Perlini and I sat on opposite sides of the conference table.

I could see April to my left. Perlini could see her to his right. She could see us both at the same time, and I could tell she planned to keep it that way. I knew someday, she'd put her ordeal behind her, but I also knew that someday had not arrived.

Perlini looked at me. "Congratulations."

"For what?"

"The official investigation has been concluded. The five dead bodies have been identified as known terrorists who died when a bomb they were trying to build exploded unexpectedly."

That little fact wasn't breaking news for me, but I did wonder how Perlini knew about it. I didn't want that answer bad enough to give him the pleasure of hearing me ask it. Instead of asking it, I lied. "I have no idea what you're talking about."

"Don't be humble. Your makeshift army performed admirably. You rescued the fair maiden, killed five of the most dangerous mercenaries on the planet, and left no trail whatsoever for anybody who should wish to avenge their deaths."

"I thought you said they blew themselves up with a poorly constructed explosive device."

"No, I said that's what the official report will say. Like your partner, I don't always believe official reports. No homemade bomb could have destroyed that cave, maybe the old Indian adobe part, but not the cave. The security doors I put in were stronger than the ones here. Quite frankly, I'm shocked that it was totaled."

I made a mental note to ask Mistress Caroline what she'd used, but I put that on the back burner. I had a more important question for Perlini.

"Why'd you warn Carl?"

"I guess I overestimated him. I thought he'd recognize the risk and do the smart thing. This is my office you know, I made it what it is. By right, it belongs to me."

I nodded. The Kiowa and Comanche own the rights to Palo Duro Canyon, the Seminoles own the right to most of Florida, ex-patriots all over the globe own the rights to family lands. The Spirits might agree, but the governments and the powers that be, do not.

I smiled at Perlini, "Sue us. If the courts say it's yours, you can have it."

"Perhaps we can avoid that. I'm willing to pay two million dollars to get back this property. That's many times over more than Carl paid for it."

"Is access to the old Federal Reserve Basement really worth that much to you?"

His laugh was not a pleasant laugh. "You're starting to believe your partner's conspiracy theories. That is almost certainly not a good idea."

I didn't bother telling him that it was the government files on Perlini that I believed this time. The government may or may not believe Carl's theories, but it clearly believed letting Sal Perlini have access to that building would be a bad thing.

"Then what is worth so much?"

"My dear boy: the only thing that has ever been worth that much money or ever will be worth that much money is even more money."

I didn't bother answering or hiding my puzzled look. I simply waited for him to continue as I knew he would.

"The tunnel below this building connects to a great number of other buildings. Many of those buildings are banks and hotels. Most of the banks and hotels have vaults that are below ground."

"Why are you telling me this?"

"So you'll see how easy life can be. I give you two million dollars. You let me back in this office. I stay here for a few months while I get set to open all the safes in one glorious stroke of profitable genius. After I have them open, one of the banks hires your agency to investigate the loss. You solve the case and find the stolen money.

"If we recover the money, what do you get?"

"I get all the money from the banks that didn't hire you and get away to my newly purchased island. I trust you understand why I can't tell you which island I'm going to buy."

"Of course, I do. Did you make Carl that offer?"

"I did, but he isn't thinking clearly. I'm hoping you two will reason with him. He's emotionally attached to this office because he thinks it made him a success. You guys know better. You know his success is because he lucked into meeting the two of you. Talk him into selling me this place and move the agency to a nicer part of town with nice, upscale clientele and a few million dollars in the bank. Life doesn't have to be hard, you know?"

I glanced at April before I responded. "Yes, life does have to be hard. We're keeping this office. You should go now."

He stood. "I'll go, but I will get this office back. It is mine by right, and I will have it again. Just because you defeated a couple of rednecks and some Russian morons means nothing. This will be my office again."

I looked at him. "You aren't getting this office. In fact, you're never even getting back in this office. When you walk out that door, you will never again be let in."

"I'll take that bet."

"It's not a bet, it's a promise."

Perlini looked at me. "I had April taken once. I can do it again. I don't think you understand who I am."

"Why don't you tell me who you are?"

"I'm a man who gets what he wants. I want this office back, and I won't quit trying until I get it back."

I thought about April, and what she had told me about being kidnapped at gunpoint and held hostage in Palo Duro Canyon. I also thought about all the things she might have not told me because she knows I'm not as tough as she is. I thought about Lamont Washington asking me if I could kill a man if I had to, and then telling me he thought I could. I made a decision. It was not a tough decision.

I looked back at Perlini, "Yes, you will."

"I will what?"

"You will quit trying to get this office back!"

"I'll take that bet, too. Why do you think I will?"

"Because I'm willing to die to keep it, and April is much too pretty to be a widow."

He looked at April. No man ever looks at April for less than a few seconds. Perlini would have been well advised to be the exception, but he was not. When he looked back at me, I had Excalibur in my hand pointing right between his eyes.

His eyes were steady as he looked at me over the barrel of the stainless steel handgun that had once belonged to the only decent man Mistress Caroline knew as a child.

"You won't shoot."

I humored him by asking, "Why not?"

"It's not in your nature. You're Carl Jennings's partner. You're both good, honest people. You don't shoot people in cold blood. Besides, you don't want to go to jail for murder."

"This is Texas, Sal. Haven't you heard of Castle Doctrine?"

"Of course, I have. I lived here. I'm unarmed. You invited me in. Castle Doctrine does not apply in a case like this."

I held the gun steady, as I tried not to wonder if decent men shoot unarmed strangers. "I'm not a lawyer. Maybe I don't completely understand the law. But, I know if I pull this trigger, Castle Doctrine won't help you."

"It won't help you, either. Would you really risk the death penalty just so your partner could keep this office?"

From my left, I heard April, "He's right, Freak. Put down the gun."

Perlini didn't move; neither did I. We continued to stare each other down.

April spoke again, more firmly this time, "Freak, please, for me. If you love me, put the gun down."

I never thought I'd hear April tell me that if I loved her, I'd do something I really didn't want to do. I always knew I'd have to do things I don't want to do sometimes in our relationship. I just didn't expect to hear her put it in those exact words.

Reluctantly, I lowered the gun. Perlini relaxed and smiled. He turned to April.

"Thank you. I always knew..."

He didn't get to finish the sentence. A nine millimeter bullet hit him in the chest a few millimeters from his sternum and penetrated the left ventricle of his heart. I didn't learn all of the details of the bullet's trajectory until much later, but I knew immediately that Sal Perlini was dead.

When I turned to April, she favored me with the first million watt smile I'd seen since she'd run the table off the break at Jeff's pool table the day she was kidnapped. As she laid her 9mm Springfield xD subcompact on the desk, she spoke softly.

"Let's talk a little about Castle Doctrine."

ACKNOWLEDGEMENTS

This one is for my father, Phil Eyre. He was one of the first people to read a printed draft of *The Freak Show Case*. When he finished reading it, he called to tell me what he liked about it. It was the longest phone conversation we ever shared, and it changed my life.

A wise man once advised authors to write about what they know. Instead of limiting my scope to the little that I already know, I try to do this by learning new things. I thank everybody who has helped me learn about what I planned to write. I especially want to thank those who continue to teach me everything I need to know about spiders without ever forcing me to look at one.

As always, I thank each waitress who brought me a beer while I wrote, especially those who inspired me, encouraged me or reminded me that playing Words With Friends won't put words into a novel. Now that almost every bar has at least five regulars who bring laptops, I am finally the trendsetter I always knew I should be.